ABOUT THE AUTHOR

DOMINIC COOKMAN lives in Canberra, Australia. He is a graduate in Law and Economics from the Australian National University. *Villains in the Night* is his first novel.

VILLAINS IN THE NIGHT

DOMINIC COOKMAN

The Book Guild Ltd

First published in Great Britain in 2021 by
The Book Guild Ltd
9 Priory Business Park
Wistow Road, Kibworth
Leicestershire, LE8 0RX
Freephone: 0800 999 2982
www.bookguild.co.uk
Email: info@bookguild.co.uk
Twitter: @bookguild

Typeset in 11pt Minion Pro

Printed on FSC accredited paper
Printed and bound in Great Britain by 4edge Limited

ISBN 978 1913913 694

British Library Cataloguing in Publication Data.
A catalogue record for this book is available from the British Library.

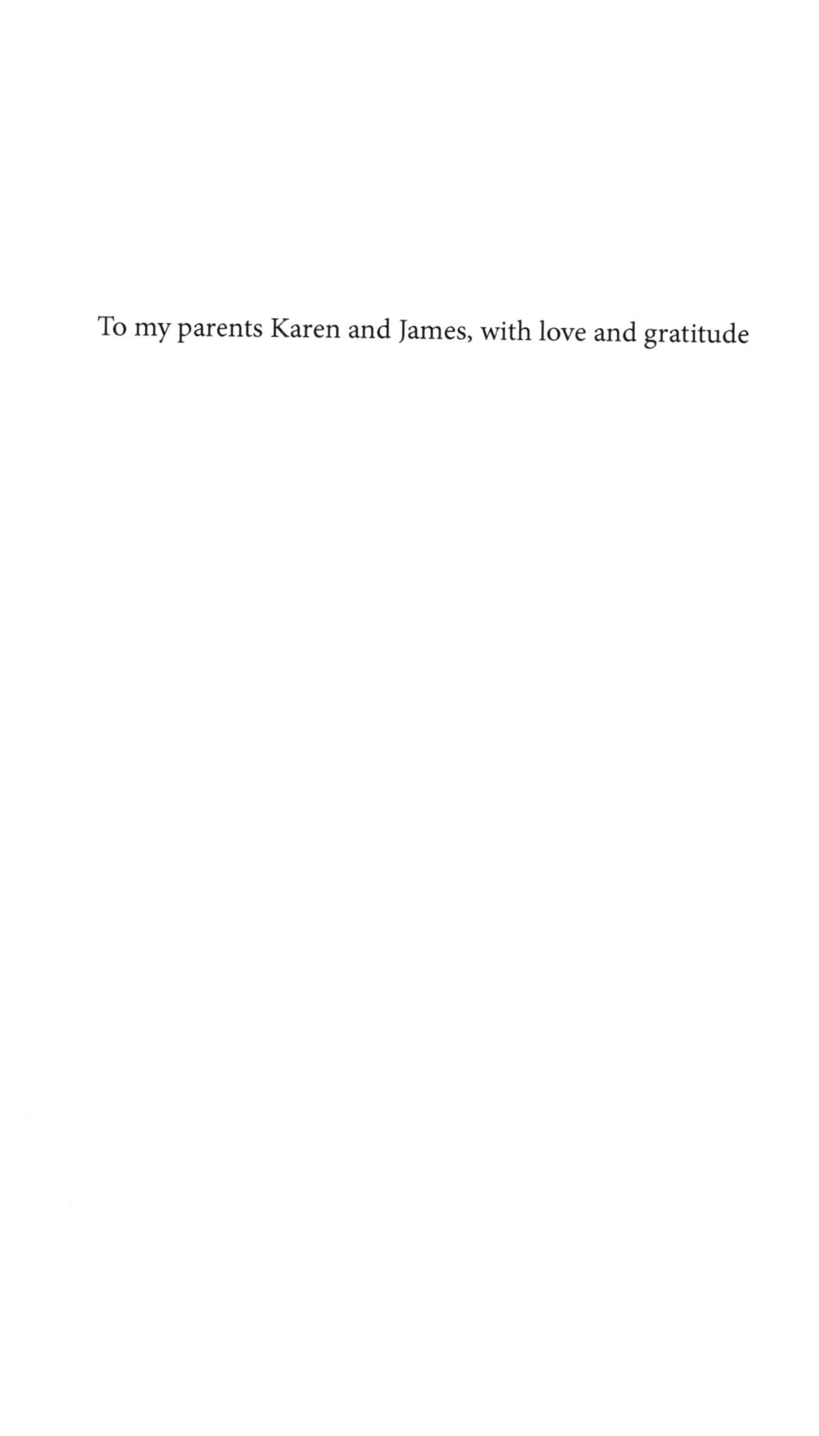

To my parents Karen and James, with love and gratitude

PART 1:

FLORENTINA.

1

London, September 5

OF COURSE, EVERYONE knew that the difficult part would be finding enough time to open the safe. It was at least – in the best tradition of luxury accommodation – tucked discreetly away in the other room. The ambiance of a deluxe suite shouldn't be spoiled by anything as crassly practical as a safe. Better for all concerned, both management and thief would have agreed, to place it in a cupboard in the alcove of the lounge room, where one could work on the dial without interruption, and where the suite's occupants wouldn't have to look at it.

Vladimir reset the dial, sat back down on the foot of the bed, lit his cigarette and exhaled slowly. Time would be of the essence, no room for mistakes, he'd lectured, to nobody in particular.

Taisia was perched on the edge of the double bed, one leg tucked behind her, the other dangling above the carpet. She looked at him expectantly, her blue eyes shining through the mist of his cigarette smoke.

Both women watched as Vladimir inhaled and exhaled once, twice and then set to work. He began to twist the dial slowly to the right and then to the left. In the concentrated silence the three of them gradually became aware of the ambient hum of the fridge coming from the kitchen and the slow drip of the tap in the cramped bathroom.

'Seventeen.'

Taisia looked bored as she typed in the number to her phone.

'Eleven.'

Taisia held the phone out in front of her, turned around, crossed her eyes and poked her tongue out to the side. A giggle escaped from Florentina and then she clamped her mouth shut.

Vladimir glanced up briefly, glared at her, then returned to the dial.

'Twenty-three.'

Vladimir pulled the door. A beat, and then: '*Fuck!*' Vladimir slapped the safe, and the clang of the metal rang out, drowning out the fridge and the tap.

Florentina flinched, but Taisia smiled and lay back down sleekly on the bed.

'The numbers must be wrong – let me see those damn graphs again.'

'Vladimir, darling, the numbers aren't wrong. Look at the graphs again.' She held up her phone in Vladimir's direction, the red and blue lines intersecting at the three points. Florentina could see this, but Vladimir almost certainly couldn't. 'We have the drill here. It's lying on the carpet. Just say the word, I can pass it over to you. But you can only make the decision once.'

'I *don't* need the fucking drill.' It was hard not to laugh at this tantrum.

Vladimir kept telling them how he approved of this work. An old-fashioned safe with a dial restored an element of challenge and problem-solving to an enterprise that still struggled to command respect in the eyes of much of the public.

Vladimir reset the dial.

'Seventeen.'

If they were stealing from another guest, the whole procedure would have been much more straightforward. Most of the safes throughout the hotel, as Vladimir could have informed you, featured a digital interface and keypad and required a five-digit code.

'Twenty-three.'

If pressed, hotel management would have admitted that there had been some rare incidents. Almost nothing that wasn't covered by insurance. Some staff had to be let go. Investigations had pointed the blame at the hotel-room iPads (also usually taken) provided to guests during their stay for providing a source of fingerprints. Once these were obtained, most of the hard work of guessing the keypad combination had been done. Unfortunate, admittedly. But again – senior staff at the Mayflower would have insisted – the problem had been identified and a blueprint for upgraded security was being finalised for approval.

It was not yet clear who had told the Prince about

the burglaries. It had been, without a doubt, one of the darkest days in the history of the Mayflower Hotel. Its most lucrative regular visitor had exploded into the lobby, flanked by two of his bodyguards, red-faced, yelling invective in English at the reception staff and punctuating these tirades with tortured soliloquies in Arabic.

The carefully nurtured reputation of the Mayflower Hotel – luxurious, elegant and, above all, discreet – hung by a thread. A platoon of managers and parent company executives were pressed into service. Rates were discounted. Concessions were made. And, in the more expensive rooms, frequented by the most loyal and discerning guests, the safes had been replaced.

The new safes, produced by a company called Aperture, were stylish and elegant, 'untouched by time, their dials will turn with the same effortless fluidity in a hundred years' time as they do today' (from the Aperture website). Their style and elegance were accentuated by their accessibility. This was deliberate. Notwithstanding the previous problems with the keypads, it wouldn't do to maintain impregnable safes when so many hotel guests kept forgetting their combinations. A good hotel manager knows when security must yield to hospitality.

'Eleven.'

Vladimir turned the dial back slowly to the left. Untouched by time, the dial moved with the same effortless fluidity with which it would turn in a hundred years' time. There was a moment of silence where Taisia sat up on the bed and looked at Vladimir intently. As Florentina stared at her, shifting her gaze between the safe and the phone, each second took longer to crawl by than the last. Florentina could tell she was concentrating hard and couldn't help but smile. The tip of Taisia's tongue had started to poke out the side of her mouth.

And then finally, finally, there was a click, and the door of the safe swung slowly open. Florentina checked the stopwatch on her phone. Fifty-eight minutes, thirty-three seconds. She had asked Taisia before why they didn't just bring a locksmith or engineer and get him to open the safe instead. 'They were going to!' Taisia exclaimed. '...They auditioned three professional locksmiths previously. Elvira introduced me and Vladimir to them, but this Prince has bouncers, bodyguards, other goombahs surrounding him. You know, protecting all the Arabs and their party people. Vladimir told me seeing the Prince can be like getting into a nightclub.'

This had been a few days earlier, before they had left Moscow. It was a Friday evening, and they were having a drink together near the university. '...And you should have seen some of these guys... dumb as rocks when they weren't twiddling a dial, and not a single one – I'm serious, not one – was even *average* attractive. There was no way we could have got them into the hotel unnoticed. And after a while Vladimir was like, "Stop this crap – I'm going to be at the hotel, *I* can look inside the safe."'

That evening with Taisia had convinced her that the trip would be OK. Taisia was so funny, and so easy to talk to; Florentina kept smiling for the whole next day at some of the things she had said ('I'm not making this up – I'm not – I had to explain to a twenty-three-year-old, a grown man, what a period was!'). Up until then she had been debating whether to return the advance and pull out of the whole thing.

'Tell me the truth – were you a figure skater in a previous life?'

Vladimir was trying to flirt with Taisia again. Taisia was looking at her phone whilst he talked and didn't respond as she swiped through photos of Lada. Florentina went back to her drawing. She had carefully traced over the ballerina's dress and was finishing drawing her hair. She stopped shading so she could sharpen the pencil again, making sure that its grey tip was honed to a fine point. She decided that the ballerina should have a bow in her hair and looked up for a moment as she thought about what type of bow it should be.

Vladimir turned back to muttering about the safe's dial, but it was clear he had exhausted Taisia's interest.

Blue was Lada's favourite colour. She took up the blue pencil, noticeably shorter than the others, and began to sketch the outline of a bow. Over by the bed, Vladimir was still babbling on about contact points or something. She hoped Taisia could understand all this, because she couldn't. She was an artist, not an engineer, or whatever you needed to be to learn about opening safes. Florentina re-traced the outline of the bow with the sharpened lead pencil.

Over the other side of the room, Vladimir's babbling drew to a close. Taisia escaped the conversation and retreated back to Florentina's desk. Vladimir was putting on his jacket and a scarf. Taisia took up a chair and prepared to help on Lada's picture. She glanced up with pleasure. They would soon be left alone.

'I have to go and meet Alexander. We'll be back in an hour or two, and he'll want to brief both of you when we get back. You two behave yourselves.'

Both women muttered a distracted 'bye' but did not look up from the ballerina. Out of the corner of her eye, Florentina saw Vladimir momentarily frozen on the spot, waiting for a better end to the conversation, and fixed her gaze on the ballerina's hair. Taisia was busy shading in the ballet shoes. Vladimir fixed his scarf and both girls could hear his awkward, uncertain steps and then the open and close of the hotel-room door.

When the door had closed, Taisia looked up, crossed her eyes and made a talking mouth with her hand. Florentina couldn't help but laugh, even though she knew Vladimir was probably still just outside the door.

'He's off to his important meeting – he has to brief Alexander and it's too important for us to come along.'

Florentina was still laughing. She glanced at Taisia as she concentrated on colouring in the ballerina's tutu. She still felt a touch of jealousy when she looked at Taisia's beautiful blonde hair, large blue eyes and long eyelashes. She was a few years older than Florentina. Every time Taisia smiled at her, or joked with her, or made one of her goofy faces, Florentina grew in confidence.

In the last few days Florentina had been daydreaming about her life when this job was done. The daydream was embarrassingly detailed: Florentina and Taisia lived in adjoining houses in a duplex. Each house had a small garden where they were growing flowers and vegetables, and Taisia was sitting on her front steps watching Florentina help Lada water some roses.

These thoughts would often make Florentina smile and her eyes glaze over. But they always evaporated when one of the men interacted with her. She had often noticed Vladimir and Alexander looking at her strangely during these episodes. Flashback to one of Mama's many warnings about daydreaming. She thought about Mama as she was watching Taisia colour in Lada's picture, and she felt a lump in her throat.

Taisia had put the finishing touches on the ballerina and was taking a photo of it with her phone to send to Lada. Florentina must have been bored because she decided to open the folder Alexander had told her to read. Taisia had been right: there wasn't much of value in it. The brief, if that was not too strong a word for it, was built around a handful of articles from websites and magazines. Three of these were in English, and she had to get Taisia to help her read them. One of these was an article from Wikipedia.

Taisia had seized the brief from Alexander when he tried to pass it to Florentina and leafed through it theatrically, before tossing the folder to the side. 'She doesn't need to read any of this – who put this together? This is useless, I can tell her what she needs to know!' Taisia declared. Florentina had to wait until Taisia had left to go down the hall before she felt that she could look for herself. Later on she had to go to Taisia and get her to help translate some of the more difficult English words.

She picked up the Wikipedia article and skimmed through it again:

'...Prince Farouk Aziz bin Fahd (born 1974) is the second eldest son and protege of the assistant minister for intelligence and armaments of Prince Salman bin Fahd.

A reportedly divisive figure amongst both the members of the Royal Family and the wider public, his aptitude for business and politics has been counterbalanced by a reputation for extravagance.

Along with his maternal uncle, Majid bin Sayef al Ibrahim, he is a major shareholder in the Qurayn Media Corporation, one of the largest private free-to-air satellite broadcasters in the Middle East and North Africa region.

The Prince owns a Boeing 777, a Boeing 737 Business Jet and a Canadair Challenger which he uses frequently for pleasure travel.'

Florentina scanned some of the magazine pictures of the second eldest son of the assistant minister for intelligence and armaments. He was a slightly chubby, baby-faced fellow, with straight black hair and a strangely unfinished-looking goatee. The facial hair (she imagined) was to offset the likeness to a schoolboy who had made too many visits to the tuckshop.

Wikipedia continued its biography (it should be noted that this article has been flagged as controversial and its content may be in dispute):

> *'In 2017 Prince Fahd stepped down from his position as Deputy Minister for Agriculture after multiple reports emerged alleging that he crashed his car whilst intoxicated in the Diplomatic Quarter of Vienna in the early hours of April 17. Two young female passengers suffered minor injuries, and Prince Fahd himself was apparently treated for concussion.*
>
> *Palace insiders have reported that the fallout from this incident and subsequent professional disgrace led to a period of professional and personal exile. Prince Fahd's professional diligence in several minor government posts led to his appointment in March 2019 as principal secretary to Prince Mohammed bin Almasi.*
>
> *On November 24 2019 it was erroneously reported by several news outlets that the Prince had been killed in an exchange of gunfire at a dockyard in the French port city of Marseille.'*

There was a second piece of information, a newspaper article, also included in the dossier. This dealt with another prince or Emirati or whatever (how many were there?), who seemed to also have something to with the oil business. Stuck to the article was a note saying 'Prince Fahd's boss may also be there'.

Florentina waded through the article:

'Prince Mohammed bin Almasi, thirty-nine, has risen surprisingly quickly through the ranks of the Emirate's power structure, and has used his growing power and influence to help shape its newly assertive stance in the region... Prince Mohammed has recently been put in charge of the state oil monopoly and the Ministry of Defence'.

The article had a photo of the other prince. He was thinner and more attractive than Prince Fahd. But there was a hard, unsmiling look on his face, which Florentina found a little frightening. The rest of the article gave a detailed account of the new portfolio of responsibilities of various ministers and members of the Royal Family. She struggled to the end, and her head began to spin a little.

Taisia was taking a break from colouring in and was browsing Facebook on her phone.

Being shut away in a hotel room like this waiting for more instructions was wearing very thin. It was such a waste of time, being cooped up in here like pets, when they weren't even achieving anything. Florentina was smart enough to keep the Prince busy for at least fifty (OK, perhaps fifty-five) minutes. Enough time for the safe business to be finished, surely? He'd probably just fall asleep after a massage.

Almost an hour later she had almost succeeded in boxing up those fears when the door opened and some of the men entered the room.

2

IT WAS ALEXANDER who came in first. It was difficult for your eyes not to be drawn to his sharp-jawed, angular, clean-shaven face, accentuated by his thick, wavy hair. He looked like he should be advertising a Hugo Boss aftershave. He glided into the room and smiled at Florentina and Taisia. Florentina couldn't help but meet his eyes and smile back. Taisia couldn't be won over so easily and pouted, asking how much more of their time would be wasted stuck in a room. Alexander moved slowly towards her as he replied.

'Is there a reason you've shut us up in this room like luggage, Alexander?'

'Patience in all things, Taisia. All the details have almost been worked out. By this time tomorrow all of London will be yours to do with as you please. But right now, right now we work.'

Florentina breathed a sigh of relief and felt her initial excitement at coming to London returning. Vladimir entered carrying a suitcase, an unlit cigarette dangling from his lips.

He saw Florentina and smiled his version of Alexander's warm, easy smile. She returned it with an icy, contemptuous look, which amused Alexander. Vladimir held her gaze while he lit his cigarette, and after a second Florentina looked past him to examine the other two newcomers.

Another man: bad haircut, cut in a circular wave so that his hair looked like a helmet. His teeth were yellowed from too many cigarettes and he threw his shoulder bag onto the ground near the bed. He was followed by a clean-cut man who came in at a march and whose posture was better than the previous man.

Alexander called the first man Yuri and they shook hands firmly. The second man took a phone call and went back out. Yuri looked over at Florentina and smiled, holding her gaze until she looked down. It was creepy.

'And who's this?'

Florentina shifted closer to Taisia, who seemed uninterested in either of the two newcomers.

Alexander was texting and didn't look up. 'Yuri, I would introduce you, but you know as well as I do that a gentleman should never introduce a lady to somebody that may turn out to be disreputable.'

Yuri smiled at Alexander's joke, but he didn't take his eyes off either of the two women. 'In that case, I'll introduce myself. I'm Yuri, and I'm delighted to make your acquaintance.'

Taisia and Florentina gave their names in the most perfunctory way possible. Alexander displayed a flash of private amusement when Yuri's delight at meeting his new acquaintances was not reciprocated. Yuri himself also seemed untroubled and, with a final grin at Florentina, turned and accepted Alexander's offer of a drink. Alexander shot Florentina a smooth, easy smile and she felt relief rush over her and her confidence return.

During the exchange with Yuri another man had entered the room. Older, grey-black hair, dressed in a button-up shirt and a sports jacket. He looked straight at Florentina and she felt a shudder of terror race through her. The upper right side of the man's face was a lifeless melted candle. Whereas his left eye flickered in its socket during the second that Florentina held its gaze, the right eye was bloodshot and its wilted iris stared lifelessly ahead.

Taisia looked surprised when she saw him. She inhaled deeply as the new man looked at her, and then turned ostentatiously back to the drawing.

The left eye looked past Taisia and Alexander, fixing itself upon Florentina. She immediately cast her eyes downward and began looking at her phone. As she blankly tapped at the screen, ashamed at having been caught staring at him, Florentina was sure that she could feel the left eye scanning her whole body. After a moment, she heard Alexander and the new man come into the room and finish their conversation.

Alexander introduced him: 'Yuri, this is Mikhail, I don't think you've met before. He's here to handle some of the logistics of this operation.' Mikhail stood silently and appeared to survey the hotel room.

Yuri: 'Does he speak, or should we change his batteries?'

'I'm Mikhail. I have experience handling logistics for various operations,' came the flat and affectless reply. 'Now run me through the plan for this evening.' Florentina glanced up again and immediately found herself staring into the eye once again, which was relaxing in its socket waiting for her to stop pretending to ignore it.

At Alexander's prompting, Vladimir started to recite the itinerary: the planned meeting with the Prince and his entourage for his farewell to London at the club (organised by Vladimir and by Sergei, who had been mentioned before), the updated reports that the Prince was planning to return back to his suite at the Mayflower where he had been living for the past three months, Vladimir's reports of the Prince obsessively shovelling money, diamonds, USB sticks in and out of the safe.

'…Yuri is here to handle the communications and tap into the Prince's phone if and when we obtain it. And I've been practising on the same type of safe for several weeks now.'

Mikhail considered this. 'It's a wasted skill if you never get into the target's hotel room.'

'Obviously there's alarms and video cameras providing security for the rooms, so we'll just have to ensure that Prince Fahd invites our guests up with the rest of his friends. He does it all the time, the whole bunch of Arab cocksuckers and their hangers-on. Sergei is confident he can steer the ship safely into shore.'

Mikhail's functioning eye swivelled slowly in its socket and looked at Alexander, who raised his eyebrows. The eye rotated back to Yuri, and then to the two women. Yuri squared his body, ready for the argument, but Alexander laid a hand on his arm. Florentina could see Mikhail and Taisia looking at each other, and an unspoken accord seemed to pass between them before Taisia looked away.

'Bring those two over here, I want to talk to them.'

A chill pulsed down Florentina's spine, and she reached out and grabbed Taisia's hand. Taisia squeezed it and then let go as Mikhail approached. He navigated his way around Florentina's suitcase and stopped at the end of the bed where they were sitting. He motioned to the armchair. 'Mind if I sit down?' Florentina nodded meekly, and Taisia answered back that he could sit down if he wanted. 'Thank you.' He sat down slowly on the armchair and looked at them both. His eye stopped at Florentina.

'So you're Florentina?' She swallowed and nodded, as he turned to Taisia. '…And you have been confirmed in your role in tonight's… tonight's proceedings?' Taisia nodded. Mikhail paused and seemed thoughtful. 'Did Alexander tell you what needs to be retrieved from the room?'

'I know what I'm doing.'

'And Vladimir – does he know what he's doing?'

'He needs time… But I've seen him do it.'

'How much time?'

Taisia looked anxious and didn't reply.

The emotionless voice repeated itself like a machine: 'How much time?'

A long pause. 'Maybe an hour…'

No reply. A shadow had fallen on the unharmed side of Mikhail's face as he sat in thought. Taisia looked like she was fighting the urge to say something further.

He ignored Taisia for a while, before turning back to her. For a moment, he seemed on the verge of saying something. He glanced back at Alexander, who had glided over while he and Taisia were talking. Alexander returned his look and nodded slightly. Alexander looked over to Florentina and winked. The pulse running up and down Florentina's spine came to a halt.

'OK, that's good.' It was difficult to tell whether he really thought it was good. 'Now let's hope they haven't changed out the safes.' Taisia looked worried, but Alexander shook his head.

Taisia looked thoughtful. 'Maybe... we could just ask him to open the safe for us.' Alexander smiled but Mikhail looked solemn. Well, even more solemn.

'Why would he open the safe for someone?'

'...Well, if... if we can get him drinking... Well, it might just be easier to...' Taisia trailed off.

Florentina froze again as she peeked over at Mikhail's face staring expectantly at Taisia. Again Mikhail seemed to be in deep thought. 'Don't try to get him to open the safe for you,' he said at last. Even Florentina, whose experience with industrial deception was relatively limited, was instinctively relieved at seeing Taisia's idea overruled.

Mikhail turned his head to look at Florentina. A strange impulse took hold of her and she lifted her head to try and stare back at him. After half a second the side of Mikhail's mouth flickered amusedly. Florentina swallowed and tried to keep looking into his ravaged and terrible face, but after another second, she averted her eyes and looked over towards the bathroom.

'It's easier to hold someone's gaze if you only have to do it with one eye,' Mikhail observed. Florentina looked over at Taisia, who nodded reassuringly.

Mikhail reprised his line of questioning. 'Can you keep the Arab busy for sixty minutes after Taisia leaves to the other room?'

Florentina nodded.

'How are you going to keep the Arab busy for sixty minutes after Taisia leaves?'

Florentina felt like she was in maths class at school. She swallowed and frowned. Mikhail had resumed his staredown.

'Well, um, after we…' The men were starting to laugh, but Mikhail continued staring at her. 'Well, with Taisia in the other room, I will give him a massage… and then see if he wants to take a shower. Then… well.' She felt herself turning red.

Florentina shuddered and wondered if she'd said enough, but she really couldn't think of anything else to add. She was becoming furious at being talked to like this, but she was too scared to push back. She squeezed Taisia's hand again.

Mikhail looked and her and smiled slightly. 'Good. Good, you'll be fine.'

'What do you do in your free time?' Mikhail asked. There were many possible things he could have said at this juncture, but this was unexpected.

'Um, well…' For some reason she was tongue-tied.

'Florentina is an artist – a drawer,' Taisia helpfully added.

'I'd like to be a cartoonist maybe… or maybe draw

posters for fashion shows.' Florentina heard herself blurting this out, and Taisia started laughing.

Mikhail's blank expression didn't change. 'That's good,' he said flatly.

At the back of the room, Alexander received a telephone call, and spoke quickly and efficiently. 'Yes, they'll ready,' he said. 'They'll be there shortly after 10pm.' He hung up, and glided back over to the three team members occupying the beds. He spoke to Vladimir.

Florentina felt her heart sink again. She had an enduring fear of being trapped having to make small talk with a stranger for an open-ended period of time. Taisia returned Alexander's smile and stood up. She turned to Florentina, winked and squeezed her hand.

Alexander bent down and whispered something to Mikhail, who frowned and shook his head slowly. Alexander turned to Florentina. 'Be well, my beauty,' he said, and touched her cheek. Then Alexander took Taisia's hand and led her out of the room. The door closed behind the two of them. Florentina was alone with Mikhail.

3

THERE WAS A small fridge in the corner of the room with a kettle and coffee bags perched on top of it. Florentina watched as Mikhail went over and began to make himself a cup of coffee. Several moments went by, as he turned the kettle on and retrieved the milk from the fridge. Suddenly his blunt, toneless voice cannonballed through the air.

'If you want me to make you a drink, all you have to do is ask.' He didn't look up from what he was doing. Florentina was suddenly conscious of herself staring at him, gripping her pencil with her frozen left hand in mid-air, like a child holding a crayon.

'Um, I'm fine, thank you,' she stammered, and she snapped her head back down to her drawing.

'You should have a drink – it will relax you.' Mikhail still hadn't looked up from what he was doing. 'I'll make you one, and put it on the table. You can drink it, or not drink it. It's up to you.' He finished making two cups of white coffee and brought them over to the hotel room's tiny table. He set them down and then went to his briefcase, and retrieved a wooden chess set.

Florentina looked at the steam curling up from the two cups of coffee resting on the table. Mikhail was starting to arrange his chess pieces.

'Do you have one of those makeup mirrors, that women use to put lipstick on when they're out and about?' Nothing in Mikhail's tone or body language changed when he asked this question.

Florentina's moment of relaxation at the inviting sight of the coffee mugs began to melt away. 'Um, yes, here...' She reached into her purse and got out the makeup mirror.

Mikhail had retreated back to the fridge to dispose of the coffee bags. 'Then next time you want to stare at someone, that is what you use.' Florentina was blushing again. 'Use it, and tell me how many fingers I'm holding up.' She picked up the mirror and angled it away slightly, and the Mikhail appeared in the lens holding up four fingers.

'You're holding up four fingers.'

Mikhail nodded. 'Good. Now try it again, but do it while applying your lipstick. That might make it look less like you're trying to spy on someone. Keep your head straight – only move your eyes.'

Florentina retrieved her lipstick from her purse and applied it using the makeup mirror. Out of the corner of her eye she observed Mikhail holding up three fingers. She concentrated on keeping her head straight. 'Three fingers... now four.'

Mikhail seemed relatively pleased and grunted to himself. 'Better. Your first proper introduction to spycraft.'

He had finished setting up his chess pieces. Out of the corner of her eye, in the reflection of the makeup mirror, she could see him take a sip of his coffee. 'How well do you play chess?' he said.

'I don't play chess.'

Mikhail paused. 'You should play chess. It's your national game.'

'Well, I don't know how to play.'

'Well, come and sit at the table and I'll show you. You can be black, I'll be the white pieces. You should hurry, because your coffee is getting cold.'

Florentina didn't particularly feel like drinking coffee, but her fear of Mikhail, which had subsided to a persistent but low reverb in her stomach, had begun climb its way back up her spine towards her heart. She didn't have any choice but to comply, and scurried over to the table. She sat down and stared at her pieces. Florentina again felt Mikhail's eye scanning over her slowly.

'OK. So I'm going to assume you don't know anything about the game, so we'll start with the basics.' He picked up a piece from his front row. 'These are the pawns. You can move them forward one space at a time, except on the first move, where they can move forward two.'

It was unsatisfactory that the very first rule of the game was immediately followed by an exception. She must have been frowning, because Mikhail asked her if something was the matter. She shook her head. 'Don't worry about it too much, just know that they can move two at the start, then one. Now…' He put two pawns, one from each side, in the centre of the board. '…When you want to take a piece from the other side with a pawn, you can't take it front on like this, you have to take it diagonally, like this.'

Florentina tried making a joke. 'What about Angry Birds?'

Mikhail shot her a look of complete incomprehension. 'What?'

'Angry Birds. It's a game you play on your phone.'

Mikhail raised his eyebrows. 'Yes, I know, what about it?'

Florentina realised that she'd used her brief shot of confidence to derail the entire conversation. 'Well, everyone I know is playing that. Maybe that's our national game now.' There was a brief silence, during which the incessant buzzing of the refrigerator was amplified.

After a long moment, Mikhail clarified the facts. 'Angry Birds isn't Russia's national game. Chess is Russia's national game.'

'OK,' Florentina replied.

Mikhail was conscious that they were yet to move beyond the movement of the pawns, and continued. 'These are the castles. They move in straight lines horizontally or vertically. These are the bishops – they move diagonally. Do you understand?' She nodded. Mikhail held up a tall chess piece. 'This is the queen, and she's the best piece you have. She can move like this or like this.'

'It's good that they made the queen the best piece. I like that.'

He nodded, and she sighed inwardly as he kept droning on about the other pieces on the board.

'Where did you grow up?' he said suddenly.

'In Moscow,' she replied, using her standard art-school cool-girl cover story. He fixed his gaze on her until she looked away again and swallowed.

'Where did you grow up?'

'In Nizhny Tagil, in the Ural Mountains. It's near Perm.'

Mikhail nodded. 'I know where it is. When did you decide to come to Moscow?'

'About a year ago when I was accepted into the art school… I worked as a model for a little while to pay for class…'

Almost true. She thought back to the last casting call when she was number 77 (of like a billion) and her anger at those losers making her humiliate herself and that piece of shit lighting guy and… she realised that he was staring at her and that she had begun to feel that anger rise in her chest again. She didn't even know why she would tell him something like that. She apologised. 'Sorry… I don't know why I told you that.' Or why he would even care. Or why she was still sitting here playing this game for children with some old man.

Mikhail was holding up the tiny wooden horse. 'Now, pay close attention. This is the knight. These are important. They move either two, and then one, or one and then two. And they can jump over other pieces. Got it?' She nodded. 'Now we're ready to play.' The lesson over, he triumphantly moved a pawn two spaces. Florentina was trapped in a board game. She moved a knight. 'Mmm. Good first move.' She suddenly felt good, although she still didn't really know what she was doing.

'So how long did you work as a model?'

After a short pause, Florentina replied, 'About a year.' She noticed herself swallowing and felt herself blush. Mikhail moved another pawn and informed her it was her move. She picked up the knight again and moved it to the corner of the board.

'I don't think you worked as a model for a year. I think you're still lying to me.'

The casting-call anger returned. She wanted to tip the whole board over and slap him. She settled for saying, 'So you're surprised that people lie to you when you demand answers to idiot questions about... nothing that matters.' The last part felt like it was wrenched out of her.

He was looking at her, but he gave no sign of a reaction. Her blush deepened, and her spine shivered. 'You have two choices: stop lying, or lie convincingly.'

There was a pause, in which Mikhail moved another pawn. 'Your move,' he said, 'Don't move the knight again. You shouldn't move the same piece twice in the opening. You have to concentrate on controlling the centre of the board. See, you have to focus on what square each piece can attack, not just where it is on the board. Understand?' She didn't really, but she decided to copy Mikhail and move a pawn.

'So are you ready to start lying properly to me?'

She was already halfway through a chess game, so she thought she may as well learn something useful from him. 'Yes.'

Mikhail moved his bishop into the centre of the board. 'Then start by getting your hand away from your mouth when you lie. Get your arms away from your throat and chest.' Florentina was exasperated. She shifted uncomfortably in her seat before moving another pawn.

She felt Mikhail staring through her again. 'You're losing our chess game. You don't have any pieces that control the centre of the board.'

Anger was fighting with fear inside her. She swallowed and looked him directly in the eye. 'Why do you think I even care about playing this fucking game?'

Mikhail's mouth curved upwards in what might have been a smile. 'So you're annoyed that I'm making you play chess?' Florentina didn't reply. 'And it's your move. I recommend that you move the knight towards the centre of the board.' She moved the knight to the centre of the board. Mikhail was staring at her again. 'You can't deceive people if you let yourself be annoyed so easily. When you meet these Arabs tonight you'll see. After five minutes you'll want to drink cyanide milkshake. So I'm preparing you, exercising your patience. Now smile like there's nowhere else you'd rather be. That's more of a grimace than a smile.'

Florentina allowed herself a mutinous glare, but Mikhail didn't react. He took a sip of his coffee and looked thoughtful. 'OK, let's take a break from chess for a few minutes.' He gestured to the bed. 'Sit down on the bed there,' he ordered. 'Now you're going to relax. That's the most important part of this job, everything else flows from it. You'll never make a good liar if you can't relax.'

Florentina slumped down on the bed at Mikhail's command. She didn't feel annoyed anymore, just homesick, mixed with residual gloom at being tormented by chess games. Mikhail finished his coffee and resumed the training regimen.

'Now, as I said, I need you relaxed. Properly relaxed, that is. Now make a ball with both your fists and squeeze as tight as you can.' Florentina realised she would probably have to re-do her nails after this. She balled up her hands and started to squeeze. 'Squeeze harder,' Mikhail ordered. She kept squeezing harder until she started to feel a little faint. She was embarrassed to realise that she has closed her eyes tight and opened them suddenly, blinking stupidly in front of Mikhail. He was right, though, she did feel more relaxed.

'Now breath in to the count of ten.' She lowered her eyes and breathed deeply. 'Good, good.' She looked back up at him and he nodded very faintly at her. 'You have to remember that. It's easy to do it now, but you have to remember to do it when it counts.' She nodded. He paused for a second. 'Now, where did you grow up?'

She looked him in the eye: 'In Moscow. My family lived in a townhouse in Frunzenskaya, not far from Gorky Park.' There was a pause, and Mikhail nodded his approval.

This set the pattern for the next hour and a half. Again and again Mikhail forced her to breathe in and out slowly, before elaborating on an increasingly complex web of lies and misinformation. He fired question after question at her, often returning to the same questions over and over again.

'What did your father do for a living?' he would ask intermittently. She had never known her father – her real father – but repetition started to strangely make her believe that he really had been a doctor who used to walk her to school each day. She did find that it was easier to be natural when you believe your own lies.

It was exhausting, and she was grateful when Mikhail declared that they should take a break. She had a drink of her coffee, and a moment later Mikhail stood up and put on his jacket. 'Come on. Let's get some dinner.' He started to go towards the door.

Florentina took out her phone and took a photo of the chessboard.

'What are you doing?' Mikhail asked.

'I'm taking a photo of the chess game to put on Instagram.'

Mikhail sighed and ushered her out the door.

4

THEY SHARED THE short elevator ride down to the lobby in companionable silence. Mikhail checked his watch and Florentina saw out of the corner of her eye that they had just under two hours before the others would be back. The elevator shuddered to a halt and the doors creaked open.

They walked across the tired and outdated lobby and out into the evening. The hotel was near the intersection of two busy roads in Southwark. He went to the ATM and withdrew some money, signalling with a raised hand for her to wait. She should have taken more offence, but the truth was she was just glad to be freed from the shitty hotel room.

As they approached the intersection the traffic came to a halt and they joined the next wave of pedestrians surging its way across the street. Mikhail took long, quick strides and Florentina struggled to keep up. She began to feel like a small child as she tottered along at twice her normal walking pace and fought to keep from slipping behind.

As he threaded his way through the oncoming crowds she saw people steal glances at Mikhail and then snap their heads back away in shame. He never deviated from his course, never betrayed any sign that he ever registered the eyes resting on him before flitting downwards to study the pavement. She admired him for that.

He steered her into a side street and their pace slowed as they approached a row of restaurants. He turned to her and asked if she wanted to eat pasta. She nodded and they went inside. The restaurant was small and quiet. A waiter showed them to a table and left them to consult their menus. Mikhail didn't want to speak, so Florentina concentrated on deciphering the available choices. The waiter took their orders (Florentina chose spaghetti), and she waited and stared blankly at the street outside.

A waitress with a sleeve tattoo brought them some water, and this roused Mikhail from his contemplations. He took a drink and refocused his attention on Florentina. 'So you're an artist then?'

She shrugged. 'Well, I go to art school… so I guess you could say that makes me an artist. I don't know… I don't even know what I want to do, really.'

Mikhail smiled ever so slightly, lifted his hand up and let it drop. Somehow this gesture made her feel better and she laughed. 'Smart person like you, I'm sure you'll work something out,' he said. In her heart, she knew that he couldn't possibly mean this, and really had no evidence on which to base this statement. She hadn't even known how to play chess. It wasn't even that much of a compliment.

She caught his (working) eye and they both smiled.

'It's good to be out and about for a little while,' he said. She smiled wider and nodded. 'Better than being stuck in a hotel room playing chess?'

'Yeah… haha.' She thought she'd risk a joke. '…That was like being stuck on the worst Tinder date ever. No offence.'

A bemused expression spread over the normal part of Mikhail's face. 'What's a Tinder date?'

'Tinder? It's a dating app. For your phone? You message people to set up dates. Don't you know about anything?'

Mikhail actually laughed at this; the sight of his mouth expanding up towards his injury looked painful, and she had to stop herself from wincing in sympathy.

'Should I be making a list? Tinder, Angry Birds… anything else that I'm behind on?'

Another couple, a young man and woman speaking English, entered the restaurant and sat at a table near them. They laughed easily together.

'Don't even bother testing me on music,' he continued. 'I've been behind since before I was in Afghanistan.'

'Oh yeah? What were you doing there?'

There was a pause. 'I was a soldier there. In the war.' The waitress appeared with their drinks.

'What war was it?' This came out in a more casual manner than she had intended, more like the way you'd ask, 'What part of the French Riviera did you summer on?' Not that she knew anyone who'd ever done that.

Mikhail sighed in an exaggerated fashion. 'Russia's war in Afghanistan? The one that went on for a decade? Don't you know about anything?' OK, she had to laugh at that. That was funny.

His smile vanished quickly, and he reverted to the grave and lifeless expression from when he first entered the hotel room. 'Who recruited you to this operation?' She thought of the first time she had met Arkady. 'Um... well, I was taking an art class part-time at university, and there was this guy there, um, called Arkady, I used to see him around...' Mikhail did not speak or react, and she stumbled over her words as she continued. 'We became friends... well... he was a gay guy and he was a few years older than me...' She felt herself blush a little. 'I, um, I told him where I was working and what I was doing and he said he had a way for me to travel and make some money... so I guess Arkady recruited me. I've been trying to get in touch with him since I got here, but he doesn't have Facebook and...' She didn't know why she shared this last piece of information.

He glanced downwards and she didn't need him to say anything further. She actually felt relieved. She blinked twice to check there were no tears in her eyes. He was good enough to look away. The waitress bringing their meals to the table broke the silence. Florentina no longer felt hungry and stared glumly at her spaghetti.

The waitress returned to the table to refill their water, and she looked up and sighed.

'So you said you were an artist...' She nodded and smiled briefly. 'What galleries do you exhibit in?'

'Um...' she laughed, embarrassed, 'I don't have any gallery exhibitions. I'm just a student... I just post things on my Instagram account. Do you think I'd have agreed to come here if I was having gallery exhibitions?' This last sentence came out more aggressively than she intended, and it was a relief when Mikhail's only reaction was to again raise his hand a few centimetres and let it drop back down to the table.

'I'm sorry…' (Why did she always feel she had to apologise to people in conversations all the time?) '…I don't know. I feel so stupid when people ask me about this stuff. And then I just say dumb things like wanting to design… fashion posters.' And now she really could feel tears coming into her eyes, and she looked away into the distance.

The truth was she could barely summon the will to check her Instagram. Every time she scrolled through it she drowned in an ocean of work and talent that was better than anything she had ever done, or probably could ever do. And here she was about to post a photo of some chess pieces! She shrank further down inside.

Mikhail had reached into his jacket pocket and produced an ancient-looking Nokia phone that she remembered some people having when she started high school. He passed it across the table to her. 'I want you to have this for tonight. It has one number in it – my number, but listed under a different name.'

He twiddled some buttons and pushed it over to her. She glanced at the screen and saw a number listed under 'Natasha'. There was a smiley face included as part of the name. She looked back up at him. 'None of the others will know that you have that. Don't use it unless you have to. I was going to recommend you memorise the number, but I thought you might have enough to be going on with

already. For any regular calls use your own phone. Don't even tell Taisia that I gave you this phone. Understand?'
She felt herself bobble her head again.

Mikhail's own phone buzzed. He looked at the screen and frowned. 'They're all back at the hotel and asking where we are. I suppose we had better hurry on back.' He started to get up and drag on his jacket. 'One last thing – although no doubt an intelligent woman like you won't need this advice. Your friend Arkady.' Another reminder of something she'd rather forget. 'He wasn't there to help you, couldn't help you even if he wanted to. And that goes double for every person back in that hotel room, even Taisia. So don't lose the phone.' And without another word he threw some money down on the table and strode out the door, leaving Florentina to hurry out in his wake.

5

FLORENTINA SAW YURI briefly, who directed her down to the hall to another hotel room. Mikhail disappeared into the first room. As she walked by she saw Alexander standing in the centre of the room absorbed in some documents.

It was a relief to see Taisia. She was reclining on an armchair painting her toenails. Her hair was wrapped in a towel and she was wearing a red dressing gown. When Florentina entered she turned her head and let out a sigh of relief. 'Finally. Somebody cool to talk to. As you can see, I've finally made them leave us alone.' She crossed her eyes and poked out her tongue. Florentina laughed and collapsed on the bed.

Taisia finished painting her toenails and started applying her eyeliner. Florentina lay back on the bed, closed her eyes and counted to sixty. When she had gone past sixty and made it to ninety-three she admitted that it was time to get up and get ready. Taisia was proceeding steadily with her makeup. 'Come on, come on, little duckling, time to get ready for work.' Florentina sighed and made a face before grasping a foundation brush.

'Well,' reprised Taisia, in between applying her lipstick, 'you haven't said much, so it really must have been bad. It's my fault, of course, for leaving you alone like that. I'm sorry. I let Alexander convince me you'd be OK.'

Florentina shrugged. 'It was actually fine. We played chess, then went to a café and ate spaghetti, and we talked about Angry Birds and Tinder. And Afghanistan.'

Taisia looked at her sceptically out of the corner of her eye. Florentina made a show of focusing on her foundation, staring intently into her makeup mirror. There was a moment of silence. Florentina edged her right eye slowly around and Taisia's face materialised in the makeup mirror. Another second went by. Then they both collapsed into laughter.

She had a glimpse of her duplex daydream again. Then this pleasing image merged with a vision of Mikhail. It felt like some sort of betrayal to be laughing about him like this. She turned away from the Taisia and looked down, pretending to search for her eyeliner pencil while she reset her imagination.

As if by telekinesis, they both switched into their preparatory routine in earnest. Florentina set her foundation, she applied highlighter to her cheeks, she started on her eyeliner. Taisia went and retrieved her dress from the wardrobe. Florentina carefully finished her eyeliner and packed up her materials into her makeup bag. Taisia's implements were still strewn over the desk. She snapped the bag shut and turned around to see that

Taisia had helpfully laid out Florentina's dress and shoes for her. Florentina felt a rush of love and knew that this must be what it felt like to have a sister.

Florentina was almost dressed when there was a knock at the door. 'Who is it?' called Taisia.

There was a pause before the reply shimmered through the door. 'It's Alexander. I have Sergei here as well. He's our… How should I put this?'

Another voice came through the door: 'Liaison to the Prince and his entourage.'

You could almost hear Alexander smile. 'Yes, that's good. Sergei and Vladimir will go with you tonight as liaisons to the Prince and his entourage.'

Taisia went over to the door. 'Hang on a second.' She shot Florentina a glance to confirm that she was now at home to guests. Florentina nodded and felt a shot of adrenaline burst outward from her heart.

Taisia opened the door to reveal Alexander and Sergei. In the background Vladimir was talking on his iPhone in a hybrid of Russian and Arabic. Florentina looked over and locked eyes with Alexander as he stepped slowly over the threshold. He held her gaze until Taisia pushed his shoulder in mock indignation. The other man stepped into the room a moment later. He was also a good-looking man, though not as striking as Alexander. He was blandly handsome, with straight close-cut black hair. It looked like he might only have to shave once a year.

Alexander introduced Sergei to Florentina. Taisia nodded to him briefly and went back to looking at her phone. Work was about to begin. 'Well…' Alexander began with his precise and deliberate intonation, 'I suppose there's no need to stay here longer than necessary. From now on it might be appropriate to speak in English.'

Taisia got her handbag and cleared her throat. 'You have cigarette?' Florentina was taken off guard; she needed more time to switch into English mode. Sergei produced a packet from his suit jacket pocket and offered them around. Vladimir finished his phone conversation and punched Sergei on the shoulder.

Alexander accompanied the group down in the elevator and out onto the street. Alexander lit their cigarettes and there was a minute of contemplative silence whilst Vladimir flagged down a taxi (no Ubers, Alexander explained – so there could be no record of their trip). The taxi came to a halt. Florentina and Taisia each took a final drag on their cigarettes and then stamped them out on the pavement.

'Vladimir will go with you two – Sergei and I have some final things to go over right now.' Alexander touched Florentina on the cheek. 'Be well, my beauty.' He winked at her and she felt a rush of nervous excitement as she climbed into the back of the taxi. Alexander kissed Taisia goodbye and she entered the taxi several seconds later. It pulled away from the curb, bearing the three of them away to their rendezvous with the Prince. Mikhail was nowhere to be seen.

6

THE TAXI CRAWLED through the London traffic. Florentina checked her lipstick in her makeup mirror as Vladimir chattered away in English to Taisia about London nightlife. She angled the mirror slowly to the right until Taisia's bored expression appeared in the lens. Vladimir paid no mind to the one-sided nature of the conversation. She let her mind wander and the English words collapsed into a monotonous hum.

The cab driver eventually interrupted Vladimir to confirm the destination and Florentina felt Taisia take hold of her hand. 'Lada got the drawing we did for her. Look.' Taisia held up her phone. A smiling little girl in a red cardigan was sitting in front of a computer with the picture of the ballerina displayed on it.

Florentina smiled and leant back in her seat. 'She's beautiful, such a cutie,' she said.

'I'm going to spoil her so badly when we get home.' Taisia laughed. She took a packet of gum from her handbag and gave a piece to Florentina.

'Have you put it on Facebook yet?' Florentina asked.

'No, I haven't put a filter on it yet. Mama's generation still doesn't Instagram their photos properly.'

Florentina sighed quietly to herself. She started thinking of home and felt glum.

'...Put what on Facebook?' Vladimir re-inserted himself into the conversation. Taisia and Florentina shot each other a glance. Florentina was tempted to relent – after all, in about five minutes they had to start pretending they were all friends. She opened her mouth to reply, but out of the corner of her eye she saw Taisia making a sad face, jutting her bottom lip out and shaking her head slowly from side to side. They both started to giggle.

Vladimir shook his head and swore at them under his breath. Florentina couldn't make out what he said. She thought she heard something about a team of doubles and making films. Taisia's expression became hard to read. She tried to catch her eye, but Taisia was lost in her thoughts.

The traffic lights changed and the taxi slid round the corner, accelerating down a side street and weaving its way through crowds of pedestrians and rickshaws. Vladimir talked in English to the driver about football and Formula 1 racing. Florentina gazed out the window and tried to relax.

She found herself thinking about a TV show she watched late at night in the break room. It was about the benefits of meditation. Apparently it helps with all sorts of things. She tried to remember what it said to do. Something about breathing in whilst counting to ten, like what she had practised with Mikhail.

She rested her head against the window, closed her eyes, breathed slowly and tried counting to thirty (she figured that she should start with a little extra given the circumstances). After reaching thirty she felt a little lightheaded, and when she opened her eyes the streetlights and neon signs blurred together for a few seconds. She made a mental note to download a meditation app when she got up in the morning.

Florentina felt Taisia's hand on her arm. 'Hey! You can't sleep yet, I need you to be looking out for me tonight.'

Florentina turned her head and smiled sleepily. 'Have you put the photo on Facebook yet?' Taisia proudly displayed her phone: the photo was posted on Taisia's feed with the caption 'checking emails'. Twenty-two people had liked it already.

The taxi glided to a stop outside an elegant building. Coloured disco lights and trance music spilled out of the doorway. Vladimir paid the driver and the two women summoned the energy to switch into party mode. Florentina checked her lipstick and makeup. She took one last practice look in her mirror, observing Taisia taking a last longing look at the picture on her phone. Then Taisia dropped her phone into her handbag, reached out and squeezed Florentina's hand for good luck, and they both got out of the taxi.

They each took one of Vladimir's arms and laughed merrily as he escorted them past the door staff and down inside the club to meet the Prince.

7

THE PRINCE AND his entourage were sitting on the VIP balcony of the club. Sergei had met them at cloakroom and took Florentina's arm as they threaded through the throngs of clubbers and wait staff. He whispered something in her ear, but all she could hear was an atonal shout and she just turned to him and nodded politely. Taisia and Vladimir were ahead of them, separated by a river of bodies. As they climbed the stairs she lost sight of Taisia, and her heart had started to hammer and she breathed deeply again and then again as she reached the balcony.

Sergei had gone over to the Prince, who greeted him warmly. They fell into shouted conversation in English. Taisia was at the bar ordering them each drinks and she took a place at one of the tall tables near the edge of the balcony. Vladimir had melted away into the crowd and she kneaded her hands together as she looked out over the pulsing mass of people.

Taisia was better at this than she was. She flirted with

the barman, leaning forward and touching her silky hair ostentatiously as she paid for the drinks. She gave a glass of champagne to Florentina before flicking her hair and smiling widely as she turned around to face the room. Sergei and the Prince saw this and shared some private joke together as they looked at Taisia and Florentina.

Seeing this, Florentina had the feeling of ice sliding down her throat. He was instantly recognisable from the photo that she had seen in the dossier; still fat, she noted with a sigh. Sergei left the Prince and re-joined the two of them.

It was obvious that the Prince was becoming drunk. He was talking too loudly and flapping his arms about to make his points. He and his friends were all dressed in expensive suits. Sergei and Taisia were busy chatting together, and she suddenly realised with horror that she had started to stare at the Prince. It had taken her less than ten minutes to make a mistake as a spy.

She retrieved her phone from her purse and checked Facebook. Scrolling through her feed, looking at photos of school friends she no longer saw, or talked to, or cared about, she began to feel lonely. Maybe with the money from this trip she could move to America, or Australia, or Brazil, or Japan, and make a new start. Taisia and Lada could come with her.

She took out her makeup mirror and looked over at the Prince. He had been joined by another Arab. He would have been handsome, except that his face was cold and unsmiling. His eyes narrowed, he appeared to be scanning the crowd back and forth. The party atmosphere hadn't rubbed off on him. Looking at him, Florentina felt anxious and she snapped the mirror shut.

Taisia and Sergei had been drawn into conversation with two men from the Prince's entourage. She realised that the night's work had begun in earnest. She felt as if she should do something, although it wasn't clear what. She went back to looking at her phone. She scrolled through her Facebook feed again, but she couldn't take anything in.

Out of the corner of her eye Florentina thought she could see the Arabs observing her. It was like being back in the hotel room: impossible to relax when you are convinced someone is staring at you and talking about you. She checked Instagram to see how many had liked her photo of the chessboard, but only a handful of people had. Maybe it would look better in black and white, or with more contrast.

She would have posted a photo of herself made up to go out, or she and Taisia together dressed to go out, but Alexander had told them to refrain from social media (she figured a photo of a chessboard didn't really count). But also because she knew nobody else really cared. She had begun to think that it had been a mistake to come to Moscow (she'd never admit this to Mama), a mistake to ignore her friends from high school when she left home, definitely a mistake to try modelling, a mistake to think she had any talent as an artist... mistake, mistake, mistake.

Her despondency was broken by Taisia's return. Taisia placed a hand gently on Florentina's shoulder and whispered in her ear, 'We're about to make contact with the target. Smile and be ready.' Then she briefly crossed her eyes and poked her tongue out again, which did make Florentina smile.

Sergei appeared at the table, accompanied by two of the Arabs. One of them had close-cropped black hair and a beard. He was tall and serious. The second man was the Prince himself. The author of Prince Fahd's Wikipedia article had captured the essence of the man well. She assumed at first that his companion was Prince Almasi, the other target, but he was introduced as Ghalib. Prince Almasi was evidently tied up with some other pressing state business.

The initial introductions complete – Florentina and Taisia were introduced as 'Irina' and 'Valentina' respectively – the two men sat down at the table and made themselves comfortable. With a heavy heart, Florentina shifted round to allow the Prince to squeeze himself into his allotted place.

As the minutes passed awkwardly, Florentina reflected on how exhausting it was pretending to have a good time. Especially exhausting pretending to have a good time in a second language. She was happy that she could follow Taisia's lead. Again and again she watched as Taisia drew another man into her web. Taisia never broke character, never gave any indication that there was anywhere else that she would rather have been.

She broke the ice with the Prince: she looked fascinated at the time the Prince met Lewis Hamilton at the Grand Prix in Germany; she found it hilarious when the Prince told them about the time he was almost arrested for property destruction in Miami. It made it easier for Florentina –

who found it hard to follow the Prince's accented English over the sound of the music in the club. Behind her eyes she could float away in her imagination, thinking about Taisia and art and the future, and while engaging in this meditation she could smile sweetly and chime in occasionally to coo admiringly at his latest anecdote.

The two of them filtered through the entourage as the night progressed. Everyone was drinking a lot. The girls took selfies with the Arabs; they danced with the Arabs. They chatted with some of the other girls who were also being paid to be there. The Prince sat down for a well-earned rest while they were dancing.

Eventually Taisia and Florentina retired to the bathroom. Taisia needed to escape from the Prince's cousin, who kept insisting that he had seen her on some website.

Hiding out in a bathroom in the corner of the club, where the pounding electronic music was reduced to persistent low reverberations, the carefree and happy expression vanished from Taisia's face. For a moment she looked very upset. Florentina reached out and put her arm gingerly on Taisia's shoulder. Taisia held it for a moment while she took some deep breaths. Florentina wanted to say something, but she wasn't sure what would help.

She started to feel homesick again. Taisia was sending a text to someone. Florentina almost asked whom she was messaging, but then thought better of it. Taisia finished texting and then continued to stare intently at her phone, whilst Florentina looked around the room awkwardly. She was a little surprised when Taisia's phone buzzed to signal a reply only a few seconds later. This allowed Taisia to relax; she put her phone away in her purse and dabbed at her eyes, before whirling around and smiling broadly.

Taisia sighed. 'Work, work, work,' she said in a funny voice, and crossed her eyes again. 'Here, have some gum.' Florentina took the gum gratefully. Then Taisia took her arm and they sauntered back out to re-join the party.

Back in the VIP section, Prince Fahd was talking to Sergei in English. 'You're a good guy, I have a lot of respect for you, Sergei, even if you are a Russian.' Sergei clapped him on the shoulder and smiled widely. Taisia squeezed Florentina's hand briefly and then left to go and sit with the Prince's advisers on the other side of the room.

Florentina headed over to an unoccupied seat next to two of the Prince's Nigerian bodyguards. As she went past the Prince she leant over and kissed him on the cheek. The Prince looked up momentarily and stared at her blankly. In that brief second Florentina felt a strange mixture of disgust and pity for the man. His eyes suggested a boredom with life. Perhaps it would be best, she reflected, if tonight's thieving could be over and done with as quickly as possible, so that its principal victim could be left alone with his bodyguards and his misery.

She got on much better with the two Nigerians. Their names were Adebowale and Tochukwu (they wrote their names down on her phone to help with the pronunciation). They were tall and very good-looking, and Florentina felt warmth and excitement flow through her body as they talked.

Tochukwu and Florentina bonded over soft drinks. For about five minutes they enjoyed an easy companionship, as they traded stories about growing up. Playing football in the street after school with his friends, the ballet class she took for a while before she finished high school. Nothing remarkable. Then the Prince and his cousin declared loudly in unison that it was time for a round of Jagerbombs, and this signalled the end of low tide in the evening's momentum.

She asked Tochukwu about him. 'That is Ghalib bin Kattan, he is the…' he searched for the right English word, 'the diplomatic one, he talks for the government. He was the Prince's friend at school.' She took out her makeup mirror to observe Ghalib under the pretence of applying her lipstick. Ghalib was bent down saying something into the Prince's ear. The Prince slapped him on the shoulder and waved him away. Ghalib retreated towards the bar.

Adebowale returned and called Tochukwu away on some unspecified errand. They were both very apologetic. Tochukwu touched her lightly on the forearm and she felt quite lightheaded. Their departure coincided with the arrival of even more members of the entourage. She glimpsed Taisia heading towards the bar and determined to rendezvous with her, but she found it difficult to wade through the additional throngs of partygoers. She resigned herself to meeting more of the Prince's minions.

It was a little difficult to process it all. She met the Prince's manager of telecommunications, his manager of protocol (she didn't understand what that meant – something must have been lost in translation), his accountant (who had taken too many drugs), his personal hairdresser (again, translation issues – that couldn't possibly be right), an engineer apparently in charge of fine-tuning the Prince's air-conditioning and heating systems in his hotel room, the assistant head of the audiovisual department (she didn't get to meet the head of the audiovisual department).

The Prince's personal hairdresser was a tanned, black-haired French girl in her late twenties whose thin smile melted into disinterest when Florentina could neither supply cocaine nor inform her when Jamal was coming back with the rest of the cocaine. Florentina tried to revive the conversation, but the hairdresser looked her up and down disdainfully, and then turned ostentatiously away to continue her search.

A wave of white-hot anger crashed over Florentina, who was left standing on her own in the midst of the crowd. There was nothing she hated more in the world than being looked down on, especially by hairdressers. She knew that her cheeks were flushed and she turned this way and that, scanning the room for Taisia, who was nowhere to be found. The air-conditioner engineer came up to her wearing a drunken, slack-jawed smile and placed a hand on her hip. She batted his hand away and retreated to the bathroom.

Barricaded alone in a toilet cubicle, she fought hard to restore her sense of calm. She thought back to the afternoon chess game and her tutorial on anger management. Resting her head on the cubicle door, Florentina balled up her fists again and breathed deeply. Stupid. Why the hell did she let these sorts of things get to her like this? She wondered what Mikhail was doing right now. The image of his damaged complexion floated back into her mind. It was strangely reassuring to think about him.

Florentina was still leaning her head against the cubicle door and enjoying her meditative break when she heard the door open and a gaggle of party people burst in. The open door allowed the bathroom sanctuary to be temporarily invaded by the thunder of the dance music. The door swung closed, muffling the music and allowing Florentina to discern Taisia's voice cutting through the conversation. 'These are beautiful hair you have!' The owner of the beautiful hair took the compliment in her stride.

Florentina inhaled slowly and let the English chatter recede into an indistinct drone. She counted to twenty before she forced herself to refocus on the task at hand.

Florentina opened the door and saw Taisia and the Prince's hairdresser chatting in front of the bathroom mirror. Several other entourage members – including two men – were jostling for space at the sink. Taisia turned and smiled broadly. 'Ah, she is found! I was thought you have been hiding.'

Disdain flickered on the hairdresser's face for a split second before she slipped her mask of good humour back on.

'This is Esmerelda, she is hairdresser for his highness Prince.' Esmerelda and Florentina smiled thinly at one another. One of the men – probably Jamal – had started pouring out lines of cocaine on the bench top. The other man and one of the other women (the Prince's diaries secretary, if memory served) watched this process with hungry concentration.

Taisia had buried her distress from earlier in the night. She put her hand lightly on Florentina's arm and smiled warmly. 'Having fun?'

Florentina smiled and nodded. 'I think it will be better when the party moves back out of the toilets.'

Taisia found this hilarious and threw her head back laughing. 'You're so funny! And you look so pretty tonight!' Florentina felt herself blush.

Meanwhile the group discussion was growing louder and more excited as Jamal neared completion of the cocaine preparation. 'You know, I've been thinking…' Taisia continued, 'we should share an apartment. You could come and live with Lada and me.' Florentina suddenly felt so happy that it felt like she could have burst. She nodded her head giddily. She felt so good that it took her a few moments to realise that she and Taisia had been talking in Russian rather than English.

The cocaine was ready. Jamal took a step back to admire his handiwork; half a dozen thin neat white lines spaced evenly on the marble bench top. One of the Arab men extracted several hundred-pound notes from his wallet and distributed them like a school teacher handing out the weekend homework. Jamal's precise and unnecessary artistry was quickly ruined. The group surged forward eagerly, each member holding their currency in tightly wound sticks. One by one the white lines were vacuumed up.

Florentina had become lost in another daydream about sharing an apartment with Taisia, when she was tapped on the arm by the Prince's diaries secretary. The diaries secretary pointed to the last two remaining lines of drugs on the bench top. Taisia stepped forward and in one quick motion bent down and vacuumed up her line, then whipped her head back dramatically. She checked herself in the mirror and then turned, smiling at Florentina. Glancing past Taisia's smile, she felt the eyes of the entire bathroom watching her closely. She clasped her note between her fingers, bent over the bench top and inhaled deeply through her nose.

The next hour or so slipped by on a tide of euphoria. As Florentina and Taisia relaxed into their roles of Irina and Valentina, the Prince was becoming more sober and focused. He was often in conference with Ghalib and the engineer. To Florentina's great private delight, Tochukwu and Adebowale had re-appeared. When she and Taisia were gabbing away with the two of them, she forgot almost completely the fact that she was supposed to be doing a job.

She liked Tochukwu more and more. In the low light of the club his gleaming teeth and the whites of his eyes were highlighted against his dark black skin. They laughed together at their mutual, halting attempts to communicate in English. She showed him her Instagram feed, and he showed her pictures of his dog, a cross-breed poodle called Gamba.

Eventually, Tochukwu was called away once again and Florentina was soon consumed by another daydream, where she and Tochukwu were having breakfast in bed together, and later on in the day they went for a walk in a park with Gamba. She wondered where they would live: London, or Moscow, or somewhere else?

She was staring into her drink. A hand on her shoulder, and once again her daydream dissolved back into the hum of chatter and music. She turned around and found herself staring into Ghalib's focused and angular face. His mouth was smiling; his eyes were serious. The evening's drug intake, and the lingering after-effects of her conversations with Taisia and Tochukwu, provided enough residual good feeling to draw upon to reciprocate with a fake smile of her own.

Ghalib was speaking to her in fluent Russian: 'Irina, I don't think we've been formally introduced. I'm Ghalib bin Kattan, I'm one of the Prince's advisers. I hate to see a beautiful woman sitting without company. There is a group of us that are heading to a bar down the street. Your friend Valentina is with them also. I thought you could do me the honour of accompanying me.' He extended his hand to her in a smooth, inviting gesture. She accepted his hand and stood up, and for a moment the two of them stood bound by the fierce and reckless attraction that one can sometimes feel for a handsome yet despicable and contemptible person.

He steered her through the club, past the coat check desk and out into the street, where a gleaming black stretch Hummer was parked awkwardly outside the front of the club. The Hummer's right-side wheels were perched precariously on the gutter, a black mechanical whale that had beached itself on the sidewalk, altering the course of the schools of pedestrians surging determinedly down the street. The Prince and the engineer were waiting on the sidewalk. Ghalib spoke to them in Arabic and they both looked at her and giggled, while she ignored them and thought about finding Taisia.

Ghalib opened the door and Florentina climbed inside. There was dance music playing inside. A slurred cheer of greeting rang out, less for her personally and more as an expression of deference to the traditional welcome reserved for new Hummer passengers.

She craned her head around to locate Taisia, who was sitting down the end of the cabin on the downward side obscured by both the Prince and his air-conditioning engineer. The lopsided parking position caused the three of them to be pressed by gravity down into their seats, like a mismatched team of under-dressed astronauts. On the other side of the Hummer people clung to handles, anchoring themselves in any way possible to prevent themselves tumbling into the astronauts. The whole situation was making it very difficult to drink champagne.

She squeezed herself into a space opposite the Prince. As she sat down she heard the door close behind her and she realised that Ghalib was not a passenger in the Hummer.

Tochukwu and Adebowale were seated together down the far end of the cabin. There was no chance of climbing over the other passengers to get to them. She turned to face the Prince, who was smiling strangely at her, his eyelids half closed. She reverted back to her professional mode. 'Are you having good night, baby?' She reached out and stroked the Prince's arm. She hoped Tochukwu wasn't watching her right now.

The Prince grabbed her arm and pulled her into his

lap. His smile had a pathetic, desperate quality to it. 'What is your name again?' he slurred.

'I am being called… Irina.' She had to catch herself before she said it, although she doubted the Prince would remember in a few minutes' time, whichever name she gave.

'What movies have you been in?' The air-conditioning engineer giggled at this question and was staring at her in anticipation.

This line of questioning was interrupted by the Hummer pulling out from the curb, its two right wheels passing in quick succession over the lip of the gutter and thudding heavily down into the street. There was champagne and cocaine everywhere. The passengers did their best to dust themselves down. Nevertheless, it was good to be on the move, and there was excited chatter as the Hummer began to lethargically worm its way down the street.

The Prince and the engineer were determined to continue the discussion. 'Irina.' The Prince was also giggling like a schoolboy now. 'Irina.' The combination of the Prince's whining register and the engineer's harmonising snigger provoked the anger to begin to bubble inside her once again.

She looked down at the Prince, and using every grain of self-control she possessed, she smiled at him indulgently. 'Yes, baby?'

Their stupid grins widened and the Prince continued: 'How many movies have you done?'

Florentina didn't understand what they were talking about, and she frowned quizzically. 'What are you talking about?' She realised that she had gone back to speaking in Russian.

The Prince and the engineer responded in kind by conversing together in Arabic. She glanced down the other end of the cabin and saw Taisia chatting happily to Tochukwu. She felt a surge of jealousy and frustration at being stranded down this end of the Hummer with these two brain-damaged orangutans.

One of the baboons was tugging at her arm. She turned to face the engineer with a sigh. It was particularly difficult to force herself to make conversation with him – the operation was targeting the Prince; it felt like she was going beyond the call of duty even talking to the air-conditioning engineer. She looked down at the iPhone that he was pressing under her nose.

The phone was playing a sort of YouTube video. Taisia was having sex with two men on a couch. There was a label on the video that said 'Euro Sex Parties'. Ice was sliding down her throat again. She looked up from the phone. The engineer was giggling like an idiot and she imagined stomping on his face with a stiletto. The Prince, meanwhile, was leaning his head back and staring at the ceiling with a vague smile.

The engineer placed his hand on her thigh, leaning awkwardly over the Prince. He was still determined to show her his phone. Florentina pushed him away, sending him sprawling into the Prince's lap. 'What is your performing name? Tell us so we know what you'll—' The Hummer rounded the corner too fast, tipping the engineer onto the floor. The Prince and the engineer found this very funny.

The engineer rolled around on the floor laughing whilst other passengers poured champagne and Bacardi on him.

The Prince was still laughing when he turned back to look at her. His eyes were no longer distant and glazed over. He was looking at her with intense concentration. 'Tell me something…' Florentina couldn't help but sigh inwardly to herself at this point; it's always trying when customers want to bring emotion into a business transaction. '…Do you think that I'm an attractive guy, a good-looking guy?'

She breathed in and out slowly, smiled, and leant in close to him. She thought about the money. 'Of course, baby! You are very good-looking.' She kissed him.

The passengers around them cheered and wolf-whistled. The Prince tasted bad and looked at her with an unfortunate air of renewed confidence and vigour. The engineer was leering at them both. The hairdresser had re-appeared and was looking at her with undisguised pity, which was worse than her contempt. She couldn't see Taisia or Tochukwu, who were obscured by members of the entourage trying to stand up and dance and being slapped down by gravity. It was a low point in the evening.

The Prince stroked her hair. 'You're so beautiful, you have such beautiful eyes.' He gabbled on like this for some time. She smiled and drifted off, daydreaming about using the money to hire space in a studio when this job was over. The engineer had reached the limit of his tolerance for an outsider monopolising the Prince's attention. He tugged on the Prince's sleeve (like a little boy interrupting his mama, Florentina thought with a smirk), and finally managed to steal the Prince's attention away.

Florentina took the opportunity to scan for Taisia again. Through the web of arms and legs she caught a fleeting glimpse of the shimmering blonde hair and Taisia wearing a relaxed, warm expression. It wasn't possible to make out who she was talking to. She gave up her surveillance and leant her head back against her seat. The Prince and his engineer were still preoccupied with their gossip session when the Hummer began to slow and squirm its way onto a vacant section of the sidewalk. The front two wheels and the back-left wheel jolted their way onto the pavement, before the engine shuddered off.

Everyone was happy to be finished with partying in transit and ready to resume partying on solid ground. The doors were opened and the revellers spilled out onto the street. Florentina took the Prince's hand and they squeezed their way out the vehicle door. She saw Taisia disappearing into the lobby with the rest of the entourage.

The party cascaded noisily through the lobby of the Mayflower Hotel. Florentina glimpsed Taisia fleetingly as the elevator doors closed shut on her and the other members of the advance landing party. The engineer had darted forward and forced his way into the elevator car at the last second, whilst Florentina and the Prince were still waddling slowly through the lobby. The Prince began to paw at her and she missed Taisia terribly.

The hotel reception staff were tactfully ignoring the steadily increasing volume of the guests who remained. The hairdresser and her underlings were talking some excited gobbledegook in a mixture of French and English that Florentina couldn't follow. Ghalib had re-appeared in the midst of the entourage. She saw him before the Prince did (who was being let down by his peripheral vision and cognitive function). He smiled warmly at her, before placing a hand on the Prince's shoulder and guiding him away for a private conversation.

Her mind drifted as she hovered about on the edge of the group, waiting for the elevator to return. It was still a pretty good deal, all things considered. Ten thousand American dollars upfront (it was nice that they didn't try to pay in roubles), plus another twenty thousand upon return to Moscow. Again and again she had turned over various configurations of how to spend thirty thousand American dollars in her mind. It was enough to leave her crappy apartment – leave Russia! – and make a new life for herself anywhere else.

The image of living in a duplex with Taisia and Lada returned. Or they could live by the beach in Australia, or in Paris, or... But she knew she couldn't leave Mama behind on her own to trudge through the snow to and from work each day. Her heart sank a little as her daydreams of completing art school in a tropical paradise faded away. She consoled herself with idea of buying Mama a small dog when she returned home.

She had taken the opportunity to check her phone and began digging around in her handbag whilst the Prince and Ghalib conferred. 'Natasha' had texted during the Hummer ride:

Text back a progress update if possible.

She glanced up at the rest of the group, but everyone else was absorbed in their own conversations and nobody was paying her any attention. She texted back:

In the hotel lobby with Prince.

She wasn't in the mood to provide more detail. She hoped that he didn't text back asking her where Taisia was. The elevator returned empty to the lobby. Ghalib and the Prince had finished their conversation, and Ghalib was again leaving the group to make his way to some unspecified destination.

She flicked her head back down to look at her phone as she felt the Prince gape at her drunkenly. He shuffled across the lobby like an injured crab, and his lopsided grin re-appeared across his face. He reached out to place a hand on her hip, but he tripped over his own feet and stumbled into her. She fell to the ground as the Prince mumbled out some garbled Arab words.

Lying on the lobby floor, she sighed heavily once again as the Prince extended his stubby chicken wing of an arm down towards her. Florentina ignored the proffered hand and slowly got back to her feet. As she faced away from the Prince for a few seconds, she allowed herself a scowl of contempt. She then got to her feet and turned to the Prince, and with a sexy smile she beckoned him to step into the elevator.

8

TIME SLOWED DOWN as the elevator ascended quietly to the penthouse floor. The Prince was looking through her, his head leaning against the wall above the elevator panel. She smiled vacantly as his jibber jabber steamrolled on, and let her thoughts float back to the first time she had been introduced to Taisia.

Arkady had arranged to meet her at the Teatralnaya subway station. It was difficult to conjure up his face in her memory, their illusory friendship already feeling like it had taken place in another lifetime. It was fun to gab about junk TV (*Russian Dolls*, *Project Runway* in America) to pretend to be scandalised when he teased her about how she must fantasise about her teachers. When the two of them walked alone down a relatively empty side street, Arkady noticeably relaxed; his mannerisms became looser and exaggerated. He would often grab her arm and whisper conspiratorially in her ear.

He steered her down a laneway, past a café and a small private art gallery, and into a chic boutique hotel called the Adelphi. They reached the entrance and Arkady made an elaborate gesture inviting her to go first. As she entered and crossed the lobby she turned back and smiled at Arkady, continuing their play-acted courtesies. Arkady was making a call on his phone and was speaking in English. It took a moment to re-adjust: '…arrived. We are coming up now.' He looked down and mumbled something else.

Arkady had told her not to treat the meeting like a job interview. 'It's more of a chat, just a little getting-to-know-you tête-à-tête.' He said this last part in an exaggerated queer drawl. 'You've got nothing to worry about, darling,' he continued, 'as soon as they see those beautiful eyes of yours, you'll be as good as hired.'

The two of them squeezed into an elevator car next to a cleaner and her trolley and rode up to the top floor. Arkady's advice bounced around her head, and she began to treat the interview like a job interview. She felt the butterflies in her stomach flutter faster as they approached floor 12. The cleaner and her trolley shuffled off at the eighth floor.

It was stupid to even care about whether or not she got this job. She didn't want to disappoint Arkady and embarrass Margarita, she supposed. That was trying to please other people got you. Caring about whether you were in the social good graces of a person whom you barely know and a person who sets up meetings for escorts.

She leant her head back against the back of the elevator car. Raisia. Of all the people to wander into her mind at that point. She hadn't even seen Raisia since that one time after school had just finished. If things had tumbled out differently – if she hadn't been such a clumsy idiot during that whole conversation. It made her cringe to even think about how she must have come across. And those kind eyes waiting for her to finish whatever made-up story she had grabbed out of thin air.

Now she was here, and Raisia was wherever, doing whatever brilliant thing Raisia was destined to be doing in the world. Maybe she could add her on Facebook and then send her a message... Or maybe it'd just be another way to torture herself, clicking through galleries of a life she wasn't going be sharing.

The elevator had finally arrived at the top floor, and the Raisia problem was unsolved. 'Earth to Florentina, come in, we're here, we're here.' Arkady was tugging at her arm. She swallowed hard and followed Arkady out of the elevator and into the hallway. They rounded the corner and stepped through an open door into the suite.

There were three of them – two women and a man. And Arkady, obviously. They were seated on the suite's lounges drinking tea and talking quietly. Taisia was perched on the edge of an armchair and looked past Arkady as they walked across the room. She smiled at Florentina sweetly. Florentina became conscious of how she had been entangling and disentangling her fingers ever since she entered the room. Another great first impression. The remaining man and woman were much older. They were looking at Arkady expectantly.

'This is who I was telling you about...' He turned around and smiled at her, and she felt three sets of eyes shift to her. '...Let me introduce Florentina.' She felt her fingers interlocking and she smiled awkwardly.

The woman looked about fifty; she was elegantly dressed in a pencil skirt and a long-sleeved wrap top. 'A pleasure to meet you, Florentina. I'm Elvira Dimitrievna, and this is Sergei Ivanovic, and Taisia Fyodorovna. Don't be nervous, sit down, relax. Let Taisia pour you a cup of tea.' She eased herself into remaining chair and clumsily put her handbag on the floor next to it.

Taisia finished pouring out her tea, placed a shortbread biscuit on the saucer and passed it over to her. Florentina nodded her head in thanks, and Taisia winked at her. She felt the air escape from her lungs and the tremor in her hands subside.

There was a moment of silence while she took a sip of the tea and placed the cup and saucer back on the table. Elvira suddenly spoke: 'I hate it when strangers stare at me when I'm just trying to enjoy a cup of tea.' The laughter around the table displaced the tension in the room for a moment, but Florentina was still the focal point of the conversation. She started to reach for the teacup, but her hand had started to shake again. She didn't dare try sampling the shortbread, foreseeing it crumbling through her fingers and onto her clothes.

Elvira continued: 'So, Florentina, we have heard some really good things about you. I spoke to Margarita, she's a big fan of yours. Said she'd never heard anyone say a bad word about you.' Florentina made an effort to smile. She had been waiting for Margarita's name to be lobbed into the conversation. She took her spoon and stirred her tea slowly, hoping that the interview would wind down soon. She wanted to get out of this business, not keep piling up debts to Margarita, and her posse, or whoever these people were. 'That's very kind of her,' she said half-heartedly.

Elvira read her thoughts: 'You can speak freely here. Anything we talk about stays between us. I think she sent you the detail about the compensation for the engagement.'

She nodded. Wished they would just say: 'This is what we'll pay you to fly to London and have sex with someone as part of a blackmail job.' But Taisia was smiling at her like a sister. Or what she imagined a sister would smile at you like. It made her overlook what an absurd thing that was to say.

Elvira continued: 'Do you like working for Margarita?'

She sighed involuntarily. This provoked some general laughter around the room, and she felt herself blush.

Elvira was pleased. 'What do you want out of this assignment?'

She just told the truth: 'I'm hoping for a lot of money so I can quit this line of work and be an artist.' More laughter, and she finally felt relaxed.

'Now that is the perfect answer,' Sergei commented.

Arkady, who had faded into the background for the past few minutes, came suddenly back to life. 'Now that is a relief. Someone who gets it.' He smiled at the other three: '…It's a job. Why does anyone take any job? Just say money.'

Later Taisia called her and told her she had been hired, and that Lada was staying with her mother, and that the two of them were going out for a drink together. They went to a hotel bar in Tverskoy and Taisia divulged gossip about people Florentina had met (Sergei – cheating on his wife with a teenaged waitress; Arkady – debts due to drug habit) and people she hadn't (Anna – nose job in high school). And after telling these stories she would giggle and fan her arm outwards as if sweeping these people and their problems off the table.

They took an Uber downtown and both laughed so hard when they realised they'd both watched *Botched* (Taisia: 'Oh! Wait, did you see the one with the girl who got the bad boob job in the Dominican Republic and the skin rotted and the implant fell out?').

Florentina told her about being at art school, about sitting in a library and trying (and failing) to learn anatomy, and, after too many wines, about her suspicions that the other students thought she was a country bumpkin.

At this Taisia had looked at her warmly, like Mama had done when she was a small child. Her blue eyes glinted and reflected the blue glow of the bar's backlights. 'Oh, sweetie… they're not thinking that. They're thinking: "Who's that hot bitch looking at the anatomy textbook?"'. They were still laughing when two more guys approached them. They couldn't make any conversation because when one tried to speak the other started giggling, and after a few minutes of this both the men literally threw up their hands and left them alone.

They went and danced and laughed and shared an Uber home. Taisia hugged her goodbye and by the time she entered her dormitory and collapsed on her bed in the early hours of the morning, she knew that she was destined to go to London.

She was still daydreaming about that evening and her elevator companion was still talking ('I've been looking for someone beautiful and kind like you, etc., etc.') when they finally reached the top level of the hotel. The doors opened slowly and a fresh storm of laughter, shouting and competing voices forced its way into the elevator. Florentina smiled once again at the Prince, and together they re-joined the others.

The elevator opened directly into the penthouse suite. The first thing she noticed was Taisia sitting on a couch talking animatedly to the hairdresser and the engineer. Her heart jumped into overdrive, pumping anger and jealousy through her bloodstream. It didn't matter that Taisia was just doing the job they were being paid to do. Florentina wanted to go over and wrench Taisia away from these two ghouls. She started scanning the room desperately for Tochukwu, who had vanished into thin air. It wasn't long before she felt herself being dragged over to the couch.

She collapsed onto the Prince's lap and started making out with him. She heard the room break out in wolf whistles and laughter. They stopped kissing and the Prince was gazing at her. 'I'm so glad you're here. You're so gorgeous,' he said. Florentina wanted to crawl into a corner of the room and die. After tonight she'd be too embarrassed to ever visit England again.

The elevator opened and spat out even more guests. The hairdresser squealed and ran over to embrace two brunettes (unrequested but enjoyable commentary from the Prince: 'There's Ruby, she thinks just because she's lost some fucking weight, she's some sort of Victoria's Secret model now.'). More Arabs, more women, more Nigerians – including Tochukwu! – poured into the suite.

The Prince suddenly thought it was vital to invite her to sail on his yacht in the Mediterranean. Florentina's response to this offer was cut short by two Arabs stumbling over and starting to joke with him in Arabic. The cocaine must have started to take hold; she didn't even care that they were obviously joking about her. She retrieved her makeup mirror and lipstick from her handbag. She squinted in the mirror and looked for the two people who were too good for this room. Taisia looked like she was giving the engineer some instructions. Tochukwu was on the phone near a window.

She turned and whispered to the Prince that she would be back shortly, and she started to leave. Before she could take two steps, she felt the Prince grasping at her arm desperately. 'Are you coming back, baby? Where are you going?' His friends were laughing at him, but he didn't seem to care. She held up two fingers and smiled. The Prince loosened his grip. She winked at him and blew him a kiss, then pirouetted and began to wade across the penthouse towards Taisia (Tochukwu was still on the phone). When she was definitely out of chicken-wing reach she sighed very heavily.

She threaded her way through the room, keeping Taisia in her sights. Vladimir floated past in the company of two of women who had materialised from the elevator. She beamed at him; being released from the affections of the Prince – even temporarily – made her feel nothing but good cheer for the world and all those who dwelt in it.

Before she could reach Taisia, she felt one of the phones buzz in her handbag. She had already reached into the bag when she realised with frustration whom the text was from (there wasn't anyone else who would care about texting her). Lo and behold:

> *Text if you get this, let me know if there are problems.*

She made a short inventory of her problems: I'm bored, I'm homesick, and I would literally saw off a limb to be in any other room on the planet. It probably wasn't what Mikhail wanted to hear, so she just went with:

> *Penthouse party with Prince but people everywhere :(*

The engineer got up to leave and she hurried over to Taisia. Taisia looked up at her and gave her own sigh of exhaustion. Florentina whispered, 'He's finally left you alone – which is good because it means I don't have to murder him in front of everyone.'

She thought that deserved a laugh, but Taisia looked serious. She whispered back, 'Get ready, it will be time to get to work very soon.'

Florentina looked around the room. There were people dancing to that 'Blurred Lines' song (including – God help them all – the Prince and the engineer); there was the hairdresser and her snakes having more champagne; there was a gaggle of Arabs talking loudly to some of the hotel staff who had joined the party after finishing their shifts; there were more guests sprawled on sofas watching a football match; there were more Arab men trying to encourage other women to dance; there were two guys kissing in a corner.

It was a mess, all things considered.

Once again she sought refuge in a bathroom. She looked into the mirror and sighed. She re-applied her lipstick (more embarrassment: kissing the Prince had smudged it). It made her angry all over again. Angry at herself most of all. She felt so dumb. The people out there must think she was such a fucking idiot. She should just leave. Leave right now. Forget about the Prince, and Mikhail, and even Taisia. But she'd also have to forget the money. And (probably) return the upfront payment. So she'd be back where she started. She felt a catch in her throat and tears in her eyes.

There was a knock at the door. 'Just a second!' She had slipped back into Russian.

'It's me!' Taisia's muffled voice came through the door. Florentina took a moment to dry her eyes with a hand towel. She unlocked the door, grabbed Taisia's hand, pulled her inside and slammed the door.

Taisia looked at her. She was still clutching the hand towel tightly. 'Look at the two of us. Crying in the bathroom again.'

Florentina felt a little better and made an effort to smile. 'Too much champagne, that's all. Always makes me emotional.'

Taisia sighed again. 'Well, sometimes there's a lot to be emotional about.' Taisia smiled at her and she felt lightheaded again. There was a moment of silence whilst Florentina finished fixing her makeup. Taisia spoke again: 'So what's the deal with that hairdresser and her friends?' This comment caused them both to almost squeal with delighted indignation.

Loud banging on the door had started. There was some angry yelling in English followed by more banging. Taisia gripped her hand and looked serious: 'I've found the safe. I'm ready to get to work so now we're just waiting on Vladimir to help empty the room.' The banging and yelling reached a crescendo as Taisia turned on her heel and threw open the door dramatically. An Arab barged into the bathroom and began to use the toilet immediately. Florentina and Taisia escaped back into the main living room.

Sergei had obviously been waiting for them. Or waiting for Taisia, in truth. He looked up from his phone and took Taisia by the arm to steer her into a corner for some private conversation. Florentina floated through the room by herself through the human rubble drinking and dancing the night away.

She had begun to gravitate towards the elevator. Maybe she could go to the lobby and rest for a time. She almost didn't realise she was about to walk past Tochukwu. He was seated in an armchair by himself, looking at his phone. He looked up at her and smiled. The embarrassment of the Hummer trip returned with a vengeance.

Florentina considered ignoring him out of shame, but after the bathroom rollercoaster she truly wasn't ready to face the Prince and his creepy friend yet. Besides, traversing the room right now would mean making her way back through the gauntlet of disdainful sniggers from the hairdresser and her cronies. She went and sat down on the couch next to the armchair. Tochukwu put his phone away in his jacket pocket.

'Florentina! I thought that you had gone back to your home.' Tochukwu said in his low, slow African voice. He was still smiling. '…Now that you have come back, this brings me much happiness.' Her mind was still scrambled, and it took a moment for it to convert the individual English words into a comprehensible sentence. She must have looked like a robot. When she realised what she had heard she felt such a strong feeling of love that she almost started to cry again.

Tochukwu continued: 'Are you having a good time?' She gave a noncommittal nod. The happiness of a few moments before had suddenly vanished, as she re-assessed her situation. This whole night, this whole job, was just the worst. There was no point pretending that Tochukwu didn't know who she was or why she was here. Who knew what Sergei – or worse, the Prince – had told him about her? Hell, what did that matter – Tochukwu had been on the Hummer.

Florentina realised that she didn't know what she was doing there. She looked at the elevator, and she looked back to Tochukwu, and she looked back to Taisia and Sergei talking and then back to Tochukwu.

She felt herself turning red, and her homesickness started to swirl in her stomach. Her breathing became more and more shallow. This must be what a panic attack was. She was having a panic attack; she had to go right home right now! Her breathing became louder.

Tochukwu placed a hand on her arm, and she looked up at him wildly. 'Take your time, and breathe deeply,' he said.

Florentina was still swivelling her head from side to side, expecting to see people whispering and stealing mocking glances at her. 'I don't belong here! These people hate me!' she babbled at Tochukwu. In Russian. There was no time to translate; she knew she had to go, anywhere but here. But then she'd be abandoning Taisia, and there was no way that Taisia would still want to know her if she left her alone trying to steal from the Arabs…

She didn't know what to do, except keep looking around the room in panic as Tochukwu took her arm and guided her across the room, past the two guys still making out, into a bedroom and out onto a small balcony. An icy blast of wind greeted the two of them. She lurched towards the railing and gulped in air. Tochukwu and the railing supported her as she felt her strength leave her and her knees buckle.

'Breathe slowly and deeply.' Tochukwu was leaning on the railing beside her. She felt a catch in her throat again as she breathed in. A tear rolled down her cheek. Down below on the street people were still scurrying across the face of the earth despite the late hour. She let her eyes lose focus, and the people below merged into their surroundings, the new image flitting back and forth like a kaleidoscope. 'That is good, just relax.' Tochukwu's voice was floating over to her.

Her strength hadn't returned. She suddenly felt exhausted. Too exhausted to even reflect on how mortified she should have been to be acting this way in front of Tochukwu. She put her arms on the railing and rested her head on them. She readjusted this position so that she was once again looking at Tochukwu. When she sighed it hurt. Tochukwu himself was leaning against the wall. The balcony door was still open a little way and the muffled shouts and exclamations of their companions would intermittently impose themselves on their silent company.

'Long night,' Tochukwu said, after a particularly loud interruption. They both laughed. In imitation of Taisia, Florentina stuck her tongue out and tried to cross her eyes. Tochukwu laughed.

She decided to ask: 'What is job you are doing for his highness Prince?'

Tochukwu paused before answering. He was trying to find the right words, as if he had been asked by a small child what happens after you die. 'Well, I have been with the Prince since I was twelve years old. I'm sworn to protect him.'

She didn't quite understand what 'sworn to protect' meant, but all in all this was disheartening information.

'...And you like this job?' she continued, although she really felt like changing the subject. Again, Tochukwu paused for a long moment before starting to answer: 'It's...' He drew this word out for several seconds until it took physical form as a shrug. They both started laughing again.

She retrieved two cigarettes and her lighter from her purse. She offered one nervously to Tochukwu (nonsmokers could get offended so easily by simple courtesies). He looked doubtful for a few seconds, and then took it slowly and gingerly like he was handling an object from outer space. 'It's just cigarette. You no smoke if you do not want.' Tochukwu flipped it through his fingers and then stuck it in his mouth and grinned. A breeze had started to blow and it took several attempts to light both cigarettes.

Tochukwu blew out some smoke and stared off into the distance. The cigarette glowed prominently against his black skin and the dark blue of the sky. She wanted to take a photo of him there and then, but she decided not to disturb his moment of contemplation. She smoked her own cigarette and it made her feel better.

She remembered to ask him about his dog: 'When you are travel with Prince, what person Gamba who has?' It was becoming more and more difficult to put together the words she wanted. It didn't matter with the Prince and the others, but now she was talking to someone who might pay attention to what she was saying. Tochukwu looked a little sad. 'Gamba passed away about… just over a year ago – that is to say, he has died.'

The sense of exhaustion returned. 'Sorry,' she mumbled glumly.

Tochukwu was still staring down at street below. 'He got a malady and the veterinarian had to…' He paused, and she felt tears coming into her eyes. 'I know it is stupid, really, to keep thinking about him. He was only a dog, after all. Don't know why I still tell people about him.'

Florentina knew this statement didn't require an answer, but she still felt compelled to speak: 'You are remember him because he was friend and you love.' She didn't know why she felt so strongly about a dead dog she had never met.

There were more shouts and the sounds of doors opening and shutting. Tochukwu nodded at her and turned back towards the hotel room. She hoped desperately that he hadn't decided to go back inside. What happened next, inevitably, was much worse. 'Tochukwu, Tochukwu, chuk-chuk-chuk, Tochukwu.' The engineer stepped out onto the balcony. The Prince was barrelling along close behind. Florentina turned ostentatiously away and looked into the street again, determined to enjoy the last of her cigarette. She hoped that they would leave her in peace for at least a minute or two.

'You shouldn't smoke. It's bad for a woman to smoke.' She turned rapidly on her heel to face the Prince. 'And you must stop eat, you are too fat.' The engineer in particular found this hilarious. The Prince's grin returned. Out of the corner of her eye, she could see that Tochukwu wasn't laughing. Her anger drained away and she suddenly felt frightened. She wanted to go over near Tochukwu, but the engineer was standing in the way.

The Prince and the engineer exchanged words in Arabic; she thought she could make out the word 'Sergei'. The Prince then turned and talked to Tochukwu (again in Arabic). She took the opportunity to escape back inside where she could write out her contact details to give to Tochukwu without being observed.

The room was almost empty now. There was no longer any music playing. A few of the Arabs were talking near the door and the hotel staff were clearing away the empty bottles. Taisia and Sergei were nowhere to be seen. She wondered how long she had been out on the balcony. Not that long, surely? It frightened her that Taisia had vanished. The uneasy truth, that she would not see Taisia again until after the Prince had been robbed, had become real. She tried to breathe slowly. Her conversation with Tochukwu had proven that she was in no fit state to help someone commit a crime.

There was a babble of voices as the others came back inside from the balcony. A block of concrete was forming in her stomach as she looked around the room for a pen and paper. It was a second after she had seen the desk with the hotel stationery on it that she felt a familiar chubby paw on her arm. She was frozen in a state of indecision.

She turned to the Prince, who was looking at her expectantly. Tochukwu was looking at his phone in the background. 'Your friend has disappeared,' said the Prince, the words falling out of his grinning fat face. 'She's left you behind with us.' Her heart shrivelled. Could they know what Taisia was planning to do? 'Where is she? We both wanted her to stay!'

She held up a finger to the Prince. 'No, Valentina is being gone, she come not back. Only me here now.' Again, she had to stop herself from calling Valentina by her real name. The engineer put his hand on the Prince's shoulder and gabbled some more in Arab. She thought she could make out the word 'Tochukwu'. The two of them concluded their little sewing-circle gossip session by breaking out into a thunderclap of laughter. Tochukwu himself appeared not to be interested in the conversation and continued to be absorbed in his phone.

The engineer went over to Tochukwu and kept joking in Arabic. The Prince was projecting his stupid grin over to the pair of them. She began to grow angry at the three of them. Why did she have to wait here whilst they joked around like a bunch of ten-year-olds? She was angriest at Tochukwu. What sort of person would work for someone like the Prince? Look at him, just standing there checking his phone whilst the other two fuckfaces made jokes about her. It was the story of her life. She turned and clambered over the debris of the party – broken glass, a broken high heel, clothes that had been left behind (jacket, tie, pair of stockings), an overturned chair – towards a bar fridge to fix herself a drink.

'Hey, baby, where are you going?' The Prince's voice wailed after her.

'I must get drink,' she replied, not bothering to turn around. The Prince and the engineer resumed their conversation. It was awful, really, being able to feel three pairs of eyes boring into you when all you wanted was to fix yourself a drink. Standing at the drinks cabinet she noticed a cupboard whose door had been left half open. The safe was inside. For a moment she stared down at it. The squat grey box rested insolently in its place, waiting for Taisia to open it. Taisia, who had vanished into thin air. On an impulse she took out her extra phone and sent a text to 'Natasha':

Only Prince and two friends left. Is operation still going ahead?

She paused for a second before sending. If the answer came back negative she was ready to run out of the room, out of the hotel, to jump on the next plane home and be done with them all forever. Her heels were hurting.

This decision made, sending the text gave her a feeling of relief. She placed her phone down on the cabinet. Taking out her makeup mirror, she took a look at the position of her three companions. Tochukwu was coming towards her. She snapped the mirror shut guiltily – she hadn't even made a pretence of putting lipstick on. As she turned around to face Tochukwu she heard the buzz of a reply message.

Tochukwu's face had turned hard and serious. It made her feel frightened to look at him. Maybe it was for the best that she hadn't given her phone number to him. She didn't do that often without being asked anyway. She felt far too shy most of the time. Tochukwu spoke slowly: 'Will you be alright here with…' He jerked his head back towards the other two. She didn't know what to say. She swallowed and nodded half-heartedly, feeling more homesick than ever. In the background the Prince was pacing back and forth, like a lot of brothel clientele start to do when the financial formalities are out of the way. The engineer was reclining in an armchair chuckling to himself, and Florentina wondered if she had ever despised anyone more.

Meanwhile, Tochukwu was unfurling a slip of yellow paper from his pocket. He handed it to her, the warmth and familiarity of their time together having vanished. 'If you need assistance.' And before she had time to process the moment, before she had time to beg him to stay a little longer, he had strode to the hotel-room door and was gone.

She was alone clutching the paper in her fist. The other two were starting to snigger again. She turned to face the hotel room door so she could add Tochukwu as a contact in her additional phone. She had forgotten about the reply message (she actually thought of him as Natasha automatically now):

> *Operation ready. Be in position in ten minutes maximum. Remember what we talked about. Good luck.*

Gee, thanks, you fucking robot. Just let me take off my clothes and lie down in position for you. He may as well just send her a message in computer code. He made her so angry. She wanted to call him right now and scream at him. Or march right back to their hotel now and scream right at his fucking monster face. She thought about balling up her fists like Mikhail told her to. But right now she decided she liked being angry. It was the appropriate response to the situation.

The Arabs were still burbling away in the corner. She took one last look in her makeup mirror before she turned around. The engineer was still sprawled in an armchair looking at her. You always looked at the clients on the CCTV before going into the room to meet them. You could often learn more from the monitor than the initial meeting. She had seen men sitting like the engineer was sitting now. Usually with them it was smart practice to have someone stationed outside the door during the session.

'Baby, come back over here!' The Prince's slurred English reverberated around the room. She was still feeling tired. Looking up from her phone at them, a gloom descended upon her one again. She took off her heels – a rare moment of joy from tonight! – and started to walk towards them. Time was running out so fast she could almost feel it flowing through her hands. 'Let's go to bedroom, baby, you and me should have some time being alone.' It was only because she couldn't bear to let Taisia down that she was still here.

'Ahmed will come as well. He wants to be with a porn star,' the Prince said. It took a long moment to realise Ahmed was the engineer and they were calling her the porn star.

She felt her heart start beating like a drill and she no longer had the focus to pretend to smile. She was shaking her head vigorously. 'No, baby, I want alone just with you, I no want Ahmed.'

Ahmed was looking at her the same way the people in the nightclub bathroom had been staring at the cocaine. Every second that ticked by in the living room increased her panic. She was barely listening when more words were sliding out of the Prince's mouth: 'Sergei said you didn't mind being with both of us. Sergei told me you had been paid to be with both of us.'

Behind her she could feel the door to the hotel room burning a hole in the wall. It made her so unbalanced that she didn't resist when the Prince took her handbag, put it on an armchair and led her into the bedroom. She felt terrible, increasingly felt like she was going to be ill. 'I need to get phone,' she said.

'You can get your phone afterwards,' the engineer replied. He had placed himself between her and the door. Behind her she could hear the Prince starting to undress.

The engineer was coming towards her. He was looking at her angrily. 'What's the matter? You need more money? Sergei told us that you would do anything with us we wanted.' He said something to the Prince in Arabic and they both started laughing. 'We can give you more money, you just have to wait for the end of the night.'

She started to look around the room wildly. 'No, no, I can't be here, I can't be here! I have to go home!' She was talking in Russian again. She felt herself shaking. The engineer was directly in front of her now. He reached out to touch her and she screamed at him, '*I am not doll!*'

Tears welled in her eyes. The engineer grabbed her arm and squeezed it. She slapped him as hard as she could across the face. His head barely moved. A wild rage flared in his eyes and he slapped her so hard that she could feel her knees buckle. She fell to the floor. Pain radiated through her whole body. The right side of her face was set on fire.

She was still on the floor when she started yelling, 'Tochukwu! Tochukwu!' It took a moment for her to realise what she was saying and why they were both laughing at her. They switched back to talking Arabic to each other.

The engineer was still gripping her arm. She tried to twist away, but his grip was immovable. 'Let me go!' she screamed, having switched, like the other occupants of the room, into her native language. There was more Arabic whilst she writhed on the ground, trying to escape. Her breathing was becoming more and more shallow.

The Prince had been roused from his post-party rest now and was easing his slug-like frame out of the armchair. He blurted some words to the engineer, who released her arm. She was still cowering on the floor of the room, her arms covering her face. She could feel the engineer standing over her. The Prince was speaking to her once more: 'You get up now, baby. Lie down on the bed.' She stayed where she was, huddled on the ground and shaking.

The engineer blasted out some more angry Arabic. He wrenched her arm away from her face and she screamed in terror. He tightened his grip and dragged her up off the floor; her body was limp and heavy. The Prince slurred out a response and started to unbutton his shirt. The engineer was dragging her over to the bed and she was screaming again. Tears were running down her cheeks and she was struggling to say anything beyond 'Stop!', over and over again.

'You are the porn star, sex is your job!' the engineer shouted at her. She was writhing on the ground, and the engineer's hand was still locked painfully around her upper arm. She had made her whole body go limp like a child having a tantrum. The Prince was taking off his shoes.

In all the commotion, it took some time for anyone to notice Taisia pointing a gun at the engineer's head.

Looking up from the floor Florentina saw Taisia's icy, serious face framed by the glare of the bedroom ceiling lights. 'Let her go, or I shoot.' The pistol clicked. 'You have the last chance.' The engineer began to loosen his grip.

She heard herself crying, 'Taisia, Taisia!' The Prince had started giggling and collapsed back onto the armchair.

Florentina's heart was hammering inside her. A tear was still rolling down her cheek. She looked from Taisia's hand holding the gun to the engineer and then back again. The engineer's hand was still encircling her upper arm. 'You let go of her arm or I shoot gun!' Taisia screamed at him. 'Five seconds!'

There was a terrible, elongated moment of uncertainty. Florentina, still seated on the floor looking upwards towards Taisia, could read her thoughts: if he doesn't release me, then she has no choice but to shoot. No choice but to kill him. There was not a single person that Florentina had ever hated more than the engineer. But she couldn't bear to see him killed.

The moment ended when a smile spread across the engineer's face. At the same time the grip on her wrist was loosened, and then she was released and her arm flopped to the floor. The relief she felt was tempered by the resumption of the Prince's drunken giggle.

She started to cry again. Through her tears she could see Taisia's arm beginning to shake. The engineer and the Prince were laughing together now. Florentina started to pull herself back to a standing position. Taisia was becoming angry and flustered. 'Put your hands up!' she screamed. 'Now, you, Prince, give me your phone.'

The Prince looked back at her vacantly and the engineer said something in Arabic. The two of them exploded in laughter once again.

The Prince reclined back onto the bed. Florentina was taking steps towards the bedroom door. They had to leave. The party was over. Whatever was in the safe, or the Prince's phone, or wherever, would have to stay there. She reached out and placed her hand gingerly on Taisia's shoulder. 'Taisia…' Taisia was still staring with rage at the two men. 'Taisia, let's go.'

Taisia kept ignoring her. Her arms were beginning to shake. The two men exchanged more words in Arabic. '*Phone!*' Taisia screamed at them. The men stopped long enough to watch Taisia's shaking arm. Florentina wanted to grab Taisia and drag her out of the room. The Prince started to yell something in mangled English towards Taisia and Florentina.

It was the renewed grin on the engineer's face that was the prelude to the thunder of violence that followed. She watched as the engineer's hand flashed up to grab Taisia's quivering arm and yanked her viciously to the ground. The gun flew out of her hand and ricocheted across the bedroom floor. Florentina screamed as the engineer hit Taisia savagely across the face. There was a terrible moment where the piercing crack reverberated around the room.

The gun was resting next to an armchair in the corner of the room. She was closest to the gun. She scrambled on her hands and knees towards it. She could hear the tears, screaming and commotion behind her, and she reached the gun. She had never even seen a gun – a real gun – before. When she was in her first year of school a boy called Nikolai pointed a toy gun at her. She had grabbed it and thrown it into the sandpit. Now she was scrambling inch by inch across the floor towards Taisia's gun.

Only an arm's length separated her from the gun when she heard Taisia's scream slice through the air. She didn't turn around. In a final lunge she seized the handle of the gun and rolled over onto her back and fired. There was a shriek and Taisia slumped forward.

PART 2:

MIKHAIL

(MOSCOW, TWO WEEKS EARLIER)

1

SHE WAS TALKING whilst he was thinking of the plane crash again. The plane was heaving itself off the dirt runway and jolting through the air until the hand of God forced it back down to earth. Then the right wing dipped suddenly and he saw Kabeya flung violently sideways, his head colliding with the side of one of the boxes.

The seatbelt cut painfully into his body as he dangled out of his seat. Immediately behind him one of the Kazakhs was screaming. The front of the plane crunched into the earth beyond the runway. He was showered with shattered glass and dust as the wing was sheared from the cabin. He punched the clasp of his seatbelt then he fell down and hit the back of Kabeya's seat.

He shook Kabeya until he saw the blood trickling down from his forehead. He twisted his body and saw the mangled, bloody front of the plane. He realised that the Kazakh had stopped screaming. Smoke was blanketing the cabin. His shoulder was burning with pain as he clambered slowly towards the door. One of the pallets behind the seats had ripped open, and the diamonds were spilling out of its innards.

There was shouting and running footsteps outside. The smoke was dense and thick, and it was no longer possible to breathe. He was rasping for air as he lunged for the door. The voices were right outside as he began to feel the heat from the flames at the nose of the plane.

The door was jammed and he kicked at it desperately. They were beating at it from the outside (for all the good that was going to do). The heat intensified; it would only be a minute or so before his would-be rescuers abandoned their efforts.

He seized the handle and pressed his shoulder hard against the door. The smoke had infiltrated his lungs and he spluttered painfully. With a final effort he twisted the handle and lunged forward. Sunlight and dust covered him as a multitude of black hands dragged him free.

'*Recule! Recule!*' he rasped at them, his arms flailing. He didn't know how to tell these idiots to get back from the plane in Lingala, or whatever the fuck they spoke. The fuselage broke into flames. The crowd scampered back like frightened animals. He struggled to his feet with the assistance of two men and staggered forward before tripping over a rock and falling on the good side of his face.

There was a commotion as the fire took hold. He didn't look back. He wiped some of the dirt off his face and started to walk towards the town. A man and a woman tried to stop him. '*Monsieur, monsieur! Vos camarades!*' He turned to the woman and told her that they weren't his friends. When he'd hobbled a hundred metres or so across the field, shaking off the hands that tried to grab him, he looked back at the wreckage. He was stuck in Congo again.

'...And then I tried working at a jewellery store when I was pregnant, but it was the most boring thing I've ever done.' He realised that he had been nodding blankly at her for the last few minutes and felt bad, because he actually enjoyed talking to her.

'And before that I tried working as an actress – blergh! – but I got to travel a bit so it had its upside.' Alexander had filled him in on this part of her biography. '...Anyway that's when I decided I was going to go back and study, and I did for a little while, but I had to quit when I had Lada and then there was all the shit with my ex...' He nodded sympathetically. '...And as I think you know I worked with a locksmith for a while – this old guy who lived in my building taught me because he was bored, I think, but all these losers didn't think a girl could fix their locks.' She paused to drink some of her coffee.

'Anyway, enough about me,' she said in a sing-song voice. 'Sorry, Alexander told me what it was you did, but I've forgotten.'

'Logistics,' he volunteered.

'Yes, that was it, now I remember, logistics!' she said, happy to have been reminded. 'Tell me all about logistics.'

He found himself chuckling. 'I really don't want to bore you, and it will be very boring.'

'Come on, Mikhail! I spent most of the last week playing Barbies and Polly Pocket. I'm ready for something – anything – that's actually for adults.'

'Well, Taisia… say you want to transport something from one part of the globe to another.'

A mock-serious expression came over Taisia's face. 'I'm listening.'

He paused and looked at her. 'Are you sure you want hear this?' She nodded. 'Well, it's my job to plan out how to get goods from one place to another as quickly and efficiently as possible. We're so used to being able to order anything we want from any part of the globe, that we don't think about what it takes to make that happen.'

'Is this from the brochure for your services?' They were both laughing. 'I'm sorry. I'm interrupting, when I really do want to know!'

He took a drink. 'OK, OK. So you want to move some goods around the world – say, pallets of food, vegetables and the like, from Southeast Asia – and you want to move them to Western Europe. Let me know when your eyes start glazing over here.'

She rested her chin on her fist and fixed him with an attentive stare. He continued: 'You can't just throw the vegetables in the cargo hold and fly them across the world for sixteen hours.' She raised her hands briefly to acknowledge the absurdity of the idea. 'So, you need to make sure the cargo is refrigerated for the duration of the cargo flight. But that draws more power obviously, which in turn means you need more fuel. Now either you make space onboard for more fuel, or you have to factor in refuelling stops.' He paused. She was still following. 'Now if the cargo reaches its destination, but then it gets unloaded and sits on the tarmac for thirty hours, then obviously that is… sub-optimal.'

'"Sub-optimal". That's how logistics people say something's bad?'

'Do you want me to keep going?' He put on a neutral expression to hide his embarrassment. No doubt Alexander knew that would happen. They were sitting in a café in the Tverskoy district. Pretty waitresses in casual denim dresses flitted back and forth against the red brick wall.

'Yes, definitely, keep going.'

'Are you sure?' He stirred his coffee slowly. 'You don't have to... humour me by listening to this crap. You can go back and tell Alexander that you went to see me, and you couldn't convince me to come in on the operation.'

She actually smiled at this. 'You know, that's exactly what Alexander told me you would say.'

'Well, what can I say, I'm boring and predictable.'

Taisia turned her head to the side and peered at him playfully. 'You know what else Alexander said?' He raised an eyebrow. 'He said that I wasn't allowed to leave here until you had agreed to come to London.' She winked at him conspiratorially. He had known this was coming. He looked at her gravely and searched for a way to respond to this admission.

'I know what Alexander would have said to you about me...' He paused and tapped his fingers slowly on the table. '...we go back a way, worked together on a few things...' Her pupils had dilated and she had leant towards him as he talked about Alexander.

His voice was slow and careful. '...Listen, I don't usually worry too much about offending people, and I try to speak plainly when I'm dealing with business. But...'

He was struggling to find the right words when she broke in: 'So you're going to try to offend me? Please, do your worst! I have a very thick skin.'

'Well… you seem like a nice person, and I like you. Um, I don't enjoy telling you what to do, how you should live your life, but… I feel compelled to warn you that this line of work, this world, wouldn't suit you.' Her expression hadn't changed, except for a slight upward curl of her mouth. 'I mean…' he continued, '…Alexander told me that you have a young daughter. Go back to look after her, go and work in an office, or a shop or finish your studies. Anything but getting involved with people… well, people like me.'

She appeared to be turning this advice over, looking thoughtfully into the distance beyond where they were sitting. He hoped that he had said enough. Obviously, Alexander had given her the very abbreviated version of his life story (she wouldn't have sought him out otherwise).

Taisia smiled again. 'So this is where you tell the silly girl that she's out of her depth mixing with the big bad men and that she shouldn't worry her pretty little head about these matters?'

He gazed at her coldly. 'I'll only tell you that my pretty little head didn't always look like this. You should listen when someone tries to help you.'

Her cheeks reddened and she snapped her head down to the left. At this point he knew he should have ignored the bad feeling her reaction gave him. He should have – for her sake – told her what Alexander really thought of her.

But he didn't.

He waited for another second, as Taisia swallowed and looked at him again. 'Look, I'm sorry…' He was stuck for words again. Taisia had regained her composure, although the previous few seconds had revealed all he needed to know.

'No, I told you to try and offend me, so I can't complain about what comes after saying something like that.' She took another breath and squeezed her hands into tiny fists. 'But what you should know about me is that I'm a very determined person, and once I have decided to do something, I don't ever quit.' Her little Barbie-doll visage was set in a picture of resolution. He almost laughed.

He also felt some of the previous desperation seep away. He should follow his own advice. It wasn't up to him to tell her what to do. He let a few more seconds pass. 'I admire your determination. I'm going to go away and think about it. I don't know how much Alexander told you about how I work, but I have a long-standing policy of not committing to anything immediately.'

She pursed her lips and looked to the side thoughtfully for a long moment while he finished his coffee. Finally she drummed her fingers on the table. 'OK,' she conceded, 'I'll tell Alexander that you'll be in touch, and to make the details of the operation available to you in the meantime.'

'Well, I'll look forward to that.'

Her warm expression returned, and he felt a genuine disappointment that their business was concluding. He had expected her to get up and go the second he gave her his response. But she sat back in her seat and kept looking at him. The waitress came and she ordered another tea, and without thinking he ordered another cup of coffee.

The flash of emotion that had greeted his rebuke had disappeared, and she talked happily about her daughter, who was four years old. He didn't mind, really. Where else was he going to go this morning?

After a few more minutes, she excused herself from the table to take a phone call. He sat back in his seat and exhaled. It felt – briefly – like the weight pressing down on him had been lifted. He didn't even feel out of place amongst the waitresses and the other patrons. He emptied his mind and stared blankly ahead, letting his eyes roll lazily over the café. The world – or at least this small section of it – was at peace with itself. For a few brief minutes he could pretend that he was part of its carefree nonchalance.

Outside Taisia was on the pavement talking on her phone and gesturing forcefully. She was emotional, pacing to and fro with short, stuttering steps. The waitress placed the second round of drinks on the table. He made to drink his coffee but thought better of it. He took out some money from his wallet, threw it down and walked out of the café onto the street.

The phone call was concluding: 'Don't call me on this number! Just get out of my fucking life!' She stood on the concourse breathing in short, staccato bursts. He stopped short by a few metres and let her regain her composure. She extracted a cigarette from her a pack in her handbag. She wielded it clumsily and he stepped forward with his own lighter. After the cigarette was lit she turned away from him to try and hide her bloodshot eyes.

'Sorry... I'm so embarrassed...' She turned on her heel back towards the café. 'I should go back in and pay, I have to...' He put a hand on her shoulder to stop her. He told her that the bill was settled, and he suggested they take a walk in the park. She nodded her head slightly, and they traversed the street.

While she gathered her composure, he gazed up at the sky as the sun pierced through the clouds. Couples lay together on the grass. A boy was actually flying a kite.

'I'm sorry. This is very embarrassing,' she said, blushing.

'Forget about it,' he replied. 'The deck was stacked against you from the start.' She didn't reply, and they kept walking through to the far side of the park. He shouldn't have asked his next question, really. A misguided attempt to recapture the carefree bond of the café. 'So... who else is part of this... project? Apart from Alexander, I mean.' She turned and looked at him with renewed confidence.

'Well... Alexander you know, of course. And Vladimir, who I recruited as the locksmith, because I met him when I worked in the office at a trades school which taught classes on locksmithing, which I think I told you.' She hadn't told him this. '...And Sergei, who is responsible for gathering intelligence on the target.' Gathering intelligence on the target. She actually used these words. 'The Prince will be in London next week. Some talks with Iran or Persia or whoever...' He didn't say anything. 'Sergei says this Prince is some big deal at home in the Defence Ministry. But when he leaves home he's like this big party animal. That's why he's attracting so much attention.' She stopped to brush the hair out of her eyes and take a final drag on her cigarette, before stubbing it out by at the base of a park bench.

They both sat down. He leant back and took a moment to let her gather her strength. Taisia sat with shoulders stooped and her forehead resting in her hands. The bright, airy girl from the café had been substituted with a tired facsimile. Her recitation of the plan had shuddered to a halt. He didn't press her to continue. A cool breeze blew across the park from the west, sending leaves spinning and tumbling across the ground.

He decided to try to redirect the conversation. 'So how old is your daughter again?'

She smiled weakly, leant back on the bench and sighed. 'She's four. Just turned four.'

'What's her name?'

'Lada.'

He nodded and stared blankly out at the park. He exhaled before speaking. 'There are easier ways to make money, you know. Jobs where the risk aligns more with the probable reward. You know… something more suited to your skills and experience. Not playing at spies.'

It was like the air and sunlight had been drained out of the day. She whipped her head around and stared at him, dejected, angry. 'Oh yeah? Like what? Working for shit on a checkout counter at Magnit like a lemming? Or maybe I should…' Here he could see her cheeks turning red as the anger burst onto her face. '…Maybe I should go back to doing fuck films and getting ripped off by creeps…' Her bloodshot eyes narrowed and tears appeared. Her lips were pursed into a thin horizontal line and she crossed her arms into her body defensively.

He was again rifling through his brain for something appropriate to say. 'I… I can't emphasise how… you don't even… It's crazy, you're crazy.' He laughed involuntarily and shook his head.

Her eyes snapped up to him and she stood up dramatically. 'OK, you can fuck off too. Just get lost. I've had enough of you. I don't need any more *men* trying to push me down. Go home to your kennel and laugh at me all you want. You're disgusting. You disgust me.'

She turned around before he could say anything further and stormed across the park. He stood up and then sat back down on the bench again. He looked at the clouds drifting lazily across the sky for a long while, until he realised he must have looked like some sort of simpleton. It was the girl's fault. He shut her out of his mind and went home.

2

IT WAS LATE when he heard the knock at the door. He was standing at his kitchen bench. He had tried to eat, but he wasn't hungry. He went to the door and let Alexander into the apartment. Alexander came in and they both went into the kitchenette. Alexander got two glasses and poured them both a scotch.

'How'd you know it was me? It could have been anyone at the door.'

He didn't need to reply, and so he didn't. Alexander strolled over to the lounge and sat down. 'Mikhail, Mikhail…' Here he looked around the apartment, taking in its sparse furnishings, its piles of books and its bare walls. Mikhail drank his scotch and began preparing the coffee.

'…I guess I'm not the first person to tell you this place could use a woman's touch.' He looked around appraisingly once more. 'Or maybe I am…'

'Well, what do you expect from a dog in his kennel?'

'What?'

'I should come home and be in my kennel. Those were the parting words of your colleague earlier this afternoon.'

Alexander smiled and leant forward. 'Taisia. Poor Taisia. Whatever did you say to her, Mikhail? I send a beautiful girl to you and she comes back to me in high dudgeon. I had to admit to her that some men just aren't cut out for civilised female company.' He leant back again and lit a cigarette.

'I think she just had trouble dealing with a detail-oriented person.' He occupied himself with making the coffee.

'Detail-oriented person. I like that. You should put that on your LinkedIn profile.'

Alexander was still appraising the apartment, inspecting the bookshelves and the Van Gogh print on the wall. He rose to inspect the models, taking the Apollo 11 module from the shelf and turning it over and back again.

'I thought you had a Vostok one last time I was here. I feel like our country deserves better representation amongst your collection.'

'You should write to the President, ask him to investigate.'

Alexander continued his inspection, bending down to the chessboard to examine the pieces arranged in the Kasparov-Topalov game. He plucked Kasparov's queen off the board, turning round to gauge the effect of his provocation. Mikhail ignored it and indicated the coffee was ready. Alexander waved him off and turned back to study the models. He was still holding Kasparov's queen.

Alexander Nikolayevich Gerasimov. He was older now than his father had been in Chechnya. He looked more and more like his father. Or what he remembered his father looked like. The most he could remember was a few snatched images from training, a brief conversation about his son in between the assault waves, and then loading the body onto the helicopter.

When he was discharged he made the rounds of the families, trudging up and down the country and sitting in cramped apartments and living rooms with the procession of tearful parents. This was when he was still finalising his transition in civilian life. He'd left Moscow till last, and by that time his condolences were well rehearsed.

The address given for Private Gerasimov (third last on the list) was a terraced house in Artplay. He thought there had been a mistake at first. He'd spent the morning clambering up and down tenement buildings in Kapotnya, sidestepping street fights, whores, drug addicts and vagrants. He wore his uniform (actually one of the last times he'd used it), and that in combination with his face had granted him a *laissez-passer* not usually accorded to outsiders.

Because of its location away from the usual swamp, he'd actually almost forgotten about the Artplay visit. He knocked on the door and stood ramrod straight, like people assumed military men must stand all the time. A young boy let out a scream of delight behind the door, and then it opened. He looked at the beautiful young woman, and Alexander leaning on her leg. Alexander saw him and then turned away, frightened (like a lot of small children). She took a moment to stare at him, before beckoning him forward and turning on her heel.

They sat down in the front room and the woman lit a cigarette (he didn't ask for one; she didn't offer). She couldn't have been more than twenty-eight or twenty-nine. 'Mrs Gerasimov, I'm—'

She cut him off with a peremptory wave of her hand. 'Save the condolences and died-for-his-country bullshit. We hadn't even seen him for like three years. Turns out he didn't even like girls. Ha.'

He clasped his hands together and watched Alexander, who had started playing with a toy truck. 'How old are you?'

The boy didn't look up, focusing more intently on swiping the truck across the floor from left to right. 'Alexander, answer the man.' The boy looked up at him and spoke.

'So how would you do it?'

He realised he was staring at his coffee on the bench. Alexander was still over by the bookshelf, turning the pages of the Gagarin biography.

'Do what? Go after this Arab Duke or Prince or whatever he is?'

'Yes. Hypothetically, of course. In your opinion as a trucking and logistics industry professional.' He leafed through the Gagarin book, as he leant nonchalantly against the wall. Mikhail sat on the stool at the counter and paused.

'Well… at the risk of stepping on the turf of your colleague…' Alexander laughed, 'I don't think, if it was up to me, that I would address the problem in the same way…' Alexander looked expectant. 'That being said, I think I should make the obvious point that I haven't been briefed on all the details, and my advice might change if—'

'...On the one hand, but on the other hand...' came the mocking interjection.

He smiled and raised his hands. '...What can I say? I pride myself on a scientific approach to these types of problems.'

'Scientific approach.'

'...And in the spirit of the scientific method, I'm reluctant to offer up a definitive theory unless I have all the totality of the available facts at my disposal. For example, I have some trouble grasping why it's necessary to bother with the hotel room at all.

'I mean, why approach the target on his territory and go to the trouble of this safe business – why not wait until he's in transit to the airport or somewhere, box him in with vehicles on all sides, and then confiscate whatever's needed and get on the road immediately.

'Get your man to keep you apprised of his movements, and make the necessary arrangements to take place at an appropriate location. In a busy city it should be possible to arrange without too much trouble. Cuts down on the risk of being filmed, less extraction time, less reliance on... inexperienced operatives. This is, of course, put forward purely as a hypothetical proposition.'

'You'd have to ask the clients that...' Alexander said, studying the Gagarin book intently. '...It's all to do with these sideline negotiations going on. Syria and the like, I believe. They want leverage at a critical juncture. The Prince has been appointed as a go-between for the talks about the air defence systems. Apparently you wouldn't know it, but he's very fastidious about the security of his documents. Paranoid about it. Our people have seen this first-hand. It's the one non-negotiable thing he demands wherever he stays. Anyway, His Excellency is the point man for these negotiations.'

'Who are they negotiating with?'

'It's what I think they call a "Public-Private Consortium". I know, I know, I laughed as well. The Arabs want first-look priority access for the new air-defence systems our guys have been working on – similar deals are being thrashed out with some of our other suppliers, as well as assistance reigning in a brewing Shiite insurgency in their Eastern province. In return for – amongst other things – tightening their oil supply on the world market.'

'And that assistance is within the gift of your clients?'

Alexander shrugged.

'…And given the evident complexity and delicacy of these negotiations…'

Alexander nodded: '…It's been decided that a discrete peek at the other side's briefing material could help—'

'Help our negotiating team offer the appropriate incentives.'

Smiling, Alexander said, 'See, I knew there was a reason I sent Taisia to you. So if the material can be photographed and then returned to the safe seemingly undisturbed then…'

Mikhail nodded slightly.

'…There's also the matter of the phone, which has to be copied. The thinking was, is, that a girl will have an easier time getting to the room, can then supervise and facilitate Vladimir's entry into the suite, and will then be able to act as a lookout while he works on the dial. She'll also rendezvous with the other girl entertaining the Prince as necessary. The other thing is just about extracting value. A smash-and-grab job to help unburden the Prince of some of his surplus valuables.'

'That's very kind of you, I'm sure. Bold move to do it before the final conclusion of the negotiations. No doubt some of this will be in the documentation that was sent through originally.'

'An admission you didn't do the homework?'

Mikhail sighed, and made an effort to retrieve the details from his memory. 'So what about this point man of yours… Jelavich, was that his name?'

'Sergei. Used to work for me a while back. Been based in England for the past few months. He's been part of the Prince's entourage for a little while. You'd like him.' They both knew Mikhail wouldn't like him. 'Anyway, Sergei has informed me, informed us…' – who was the us here: the usual team, the porno actress, someone else? – 'that some of the contractors are meeting with the Prince in London for final demonstrations and run-throughs before the official testing.'

He didn't say anything to that. He tipped some sugar into his coffee and started to stir. It was the same feeling from Afghanistan, Chechnya, a few other places. Like there was some time lag between the signals sent by his brain and the movement of his body. The stirring had become slower as he stared into the coffee.

'Earth to Mikhail. Come in, come in.'

'When is the Prince scheduled to leave London?'

'The 18th.'

'So that's—'

Alexander nodded. 'Yes, the day after this phase of the talks concludes. Early-morning flight home via the Amalfi Coast. Sergei tells me he usually has a blow-out on the final evening – stays out all night, escapes to the airport and sleeps it off on the plane. We all need our little rituals. We also know that he has some other side-line business during the week, for which he is expected to receive a handling fee. In liquid form.'

'So it seems safe to assume you already have canvassed my airport transit plan.'

'Correct. But without the benefit of your planning and logistical experience.'

There was a time long ago when he would have been flattered. Now it just reminded him how tired he felt.

'Well, tell them to send over the updated material incorporating what you've just told me. Tell Vladimir to come and see me. I'll work in an advisory capacity only.'

'I knew I could count on you.'

'Tell them I'll be in touch with my fee for services. To be paid upfront.'

Alexander laughed at that. He left soon after to deliver the happy news. On his way out the door Mikhail said one last thing: 'Oh, and tell the girl I'm sorry about how our meeting ended today.' They shook hands and he closed the door.

He had never made enquiries into Alexander's other

work, and couldn't bring himself to. There had been an incident once in the past. A mutual acquaintance had once sent him a brief asking for him to prepare a report on requirements for shipping containers with oxygen recycling sufficient for at least twenty persons. He'd flown into a righteous fury and stormed over to see him. Ranted and raved like a smug madman.

Alexander denied all knowledge, of course. But afterwards they hadn't spoken for almost two years. He'd worked like hell to make up for the business that was no longer being steered his way. He'd got a job organising the stocking system at a warehouse of a small department store chain through an army connection. Similar jobs followed. Very low-level things, for the most part.

He reconnected with him after Anya died. He'd sat down the back, but it was only a small funeral. Alexander spoke, obviously, but he tuned out the words and stared at the floor. The usual thing with funerals: you catch yourself drifting off and then you feel guilty because you're not devoting every waking thought to the dearly departed.

He'd trudged out into the snow with the other mourners and walked towards his car. As he traversed the car park he looked up and Alexander had materialised in front of him.

'Well, let me offer my condolences.'

'I've done my crying.'

A gust of wind blew across the lot. Everyone else was disbursing into the cemetery, dressed in black and hunched over, smudges against the grey sky. It actually felt good to see him again. He knew he should be angry with him, play the stern moralising conscience on behalf of humanity's stricken multitudes. Or whatever. Alexander wouldn't bring up the other business, and he wouldn't press.

Embarassing thought: he was relieved just to have the company. They walked through the car park and he knew that they were going to work together again. It would have been a much better solution (he would later reflect) just to get a dog.

They reached his car. He looked up at the sun trying to force its way through the cloud cover. For a minute he skirted mentally around the self-pitying vortex of thoughts ('talking to the only person left who cares I'm alive or dead – wah wah wah'). He shut off those thoughts in his mind and turned to Alexander.

'So can I count you back in, Mikhail?'

He'd nodded, and now, almost two years later, he was deeper in than he ever had wanted to be.

Taisia. What a ridiculous person. He didn't owe anything to her, didn't even owe it to Alexander. Too stupid to see what could happen to her if she agreed to participate.

He thought of that stupid girl and he knew that he was going to agree to go to London. He wouldn't tell Alexander right now. Besides, he already knew.

3

A MOTORCYCLE COURIER dropped off the parcel at 9:30 the next morning. He took it inside and dropped it on the dining table. The thud echoed through the apartment. He'd risen early in anticipation, tying up loose ends (supply chain efficiency report for a trucking company, status report on a container ship refurbishment), and rescheduling the week's meetings.

He stood for a moment contemplating the thick brown envelope on the table, before tearing it open and shaking the papers free. A covering note was included: '*Hopefully there's enough here to get you started on your day of the jackal routine. A.*'

Alexander's hand was clearly visible as he leafed through the material. There were biographies of the Prince and his relatives, and a much longer description of the Prince's summer itinerary (Monaco, Amalfi Coast, Copenhagen, Paris, London). Translated cutouts from some Arab websites about the Prince's past antics. Descriptions of the *dramatis personae* of the Prince's staff and inner circle, brochures, blueprints for the Mayflower hotel.

Some of the material was surprisingly devoted to a recount of the diplomatic negotiations over the S-400 missile defence system. He'd forgotten about the Prince's role in the Defence Ministry. He wondered if this had been placed in the package by mistake, and how the clients would feel about him seeing this material (not that he cared). In truth, the safe wasn't his responsibility, and after the denouement of yesterday's lunch he was happy for it to stay that way.

There was an additional folder dealing with the route from the hotel to the private airfield. Google Maps readouts, traffic flow reports, photographs of the freeway. He made a note to order research on scheduled roadworks and maintenance. He read and re-read the traffic reports, and looked online for the Google Earth photos of the approach to the airfield.

There was no information given about the vehicles to be used, or more importantly the hold-up men. What weapons were going to be used, and where were they going to be sourced? Where were the vehicles going to be disposed of at the conclusion of the hit? And how? How many vehicles did they have, and how would the drivers communicate securely? Had the plan been rehearsed, and if so when?

He checked and double-checked the folders for answers. Eventually he threw down his pen in rage and frustration.

It was ten minutes before he had calmed down enough

to call Alexander. He had sat on his lounge taking three deep breaths at a time like he was in some goddamned yoga class. He called Alexander and said there was a folder missing. No, there were only supposed to be three folders. Then your planners haven't done their job.

Alexander, laughing: 'I'm sending someone to pick you up.'

'Be ready to work.' He rang off.

The car came twenty minutes later and took him across town to Alexander's apartment. He took the elevator upstairs and walked in without knocking. Alexander was sitting at his desk and another man was seated on the couch, who turned and looked up at him. He couldn't remember his name.

'No knock? He could have been jerking off in here.'

He threw down the folders and they fanned out over the table. 'I'll knock next time in case you're jerking him off.'

Alexander was smiling as he leafed through the paperwork. 'I think you know Vladimir – locksmith – advising on the safe requirements.' Here he looked at Vladimir, gut spilling out of jeans, dishevelled. '…He knows what to do – open the safe, swap out the USB stick, photograph any documents, close the safe. Taisia will be acting as the liaison for the evening, overseeing the interaction between our other personnel and the Prince and his people, assisting where necessary with the safe. The Prince never ever travels light and the final part of the operation is to relieve him of some of that surplus baggage.'

Alexander raised his hand, signalling that he had rested his case on this issue. Mikhail was done talking to

Vladimir and sat down at the dining table with the red folder.

'Let's start with the airfield route.'

Vladimir left soon after, and the two of them worked solidly for the next twelve hours. The vehicles were the first problem. Alexander had actually signed off on four hire cars from a dealership in the outer suburbs of London. As soon as the words came out of his mouth Alexander realised the mistake. They instructed Alexander's people in London to buy five junk four-wheel drives through one of the shell companies immediately. They hired a further five sedans which would collect the personnel after the dust had cleared.

They rang Sergei over an encrypted channel and had a long teleconference about the Prince's convoy (five to seven cars), a description of his private jet (2002 Gulfstream G550, reserved hangar at London Luton Airport), his staff (diplomatic aides, bodyguards, personal staff).

They worked backwards along the route from the airport back to the hotel. They double-checked the public works schedule to confirm there were no roadworks along either possible approach road. Both approaches were bisected by Chiltern Green Road. Long-stay parking was available nearby, and they booked five spaces at three different lots. There was a landfill about twenty kilometres west of the intersection, connected by a single road. They sent through instructions to the scouts to confirm it was suitable for the vehicle changeover.

The weapons (mainly Ruger AR-556s) were sourced from local contacts in London. Photographic evidence was sent through to prove the serial numbers had been dissolved using acid (probably overkill, as they would be disassembled and transported out of the country on a shipping container immediately after the operation).

The men came from the usual places. South Africans, veterans of the French Foreign Legion, some ex-Spetsnaz. Alexander had used some of them for bodyguards at a product handover, and obliquely mentioned that they had been put to work on some other projects. He glanced over the list briefly, but it wasn't his job to vet the personnel, and there wasn't any time to change them out anyway.

'They've been rehearsing the intercept for the past week.'

'Rehearsing? What, like it's a fucking ballet recital?'

'Well.'

They were laughing. Alexander brought in the team leader later in the afternoon. A reserved and intelligent ex-French Legionnaire from St Petersburg who went by Max, Mikhail liked him immediately. Alexander gave Max the summary of the day's work. Max listened carefully. He asked some questions about the traffic-light timings around Chiltern Green Road.

Mikhail had looked up the indicative timings but emphasised that (obviously) the pressure pads might change this. There wasn't any time to explore tapping into the system to alter the timings. Alexander and Max were discussing the extraction of the material once the cars had been halted.

Mikhail was thinking and excused himself for a few minutes. He made a few calls and came back and told the other two that he had an order confirmed for two semi-trailers (and containers) often used by an overnight courier company. They had to get Max to ring some of his men and confirm he had at least two qualified drivers.

There was an anxious wait while Max rung round trying to work out if they would need to find another driver in the next twenty-four hours. It transpired that one of the men had worked construction driving a cement mixer in Warsaw before going into the Legion. He had a friend who was a crane operator who could drive the other truck. Alexander had said yes before Mikhail or Max could give an opinion.

Mikhail started to remonstrate with Alexander, who retorted (not unreasonably, it had to be admitted) that unless Mikhail was volunteering to drive the other truck himself then they didn't have much of a choice at this point. Max nodded hesitantly.

'Besides, he only has to lurch it forward a few hundred metres and then brake.' Max looked down at the floor worriedly.

'Get your friend the cement-truck driver to send us some video of him driving. If things are desperate I can drive the truck,' Mikhail said.

'It's your job to ensure things don't get desperate,' replied Alexander.

It was meant as a joke, but he felt himself growing angry. He looked up at Alexander blankly. Alexander read his expression, and – in a gesture strikingly reminiscent of the Barbie doll at lunchtime – swept his arm outward from his body, erasing any possible objections. It had been the same ever since he'd brought Alexander in years ago, connecting him with the contacts from the army, the prisons and even acting as a sounding board for his first few operations.

Max was concluding a phone call with one of his other men about the walkie-talkie app they had all downloaded to communicate. He realised he had been staring out the window like a ghost.

Alexander: 'Let's get lunch.' He nodded, and they went down the stairs and out of the building into the afternoon. A breeze was blowing and they walked in silence as Alexander texted. He watched some leaves blowing across the street and felt despondent.

4

THE NEXT THREE days were a blur of meetings, phone calls, arguments and research. Alexander spent a lot of time on the phone with the sources in the Prince's circle who were feeding back details of the arrangements for the talks and updates to the itinerary.

There was word that another girl – some university student – had been recruited to come to London. He was still keeping a distance from that part of the operation. Someone somewhere along the line was convinced of the necessity of obtaining the Prince's phone. He still hadn't enquired into the connection between Alexander and whatever directorate had placed the order for the surveillance.

He'd get home late at night and find himself turning over the lunch with Taisia in his mind. Alone staring at his silhouetted reflection in the kitchenette window, he'd think about how stupid and embarrassing it was. First woman that has a coffee with you and you're like some idiot thirteen-year-old school student with a crush on a girl in math class. He was ashamed to be devoting any thought to some porn-star whore or whoever she was.

The day before the flight out was warm and clear. He'd had a final conference with Alexander and Max in the morning and then told them he would be unavailable for the afternoon.

He ate a sandwich at home. Afterward he tried reading a memoir about neurosurgery, but then gave up and left the apartment and walked around downtown. He wandered in and out of boutiques in Tverskaya. After the toy-shop assistant had helped him find a Polly Pocket (whatever that was) he found himself staring at his coffee, stirring slowly.

He realised he'd just bought an expensive toy for a young child he'd never met, whose mother hated him. Well, not that expensive. But still. It actually made him laugh. He finished his coffee and strolled home in the lengthening shadows smiling to himself. Alone in his apartment that evening he re-packed his suitcase again, and then heated up a frozen meal and sat at the table eating in silence and staring disconsolately at the living room wall.

For a few minutes he logged into the secure app and scrolled through the latest messages. Yuri and Ivan were ribbing Alexander about the girl: ('Make sure you triple bag it with that gash.' 'She's a serious actress – she can act with twenty guys all day long.')

He slid the phone across the table and slumped further into despondency. For a minute or two he turned the 'Polly Pocket™ Beach Vibes Backpack™' toy around in his hands. The good feelings of his walk home had slipped away. It had been a long time since he'd felt like this, certainly since before he stopped drinking.

For a few moments he thought about not showing up at the airport in the next morning. He could return the fee (painful as that would be). Keep doing what he had been doing since the crash – the low-level freelance reports for distribution warehouses, cut-price office-supply chains and whatever his army contacts threw his way. Or he could just go and work at Magnit like a fucking lemming.

Since Chechnya he had been to – here he started to count the funerals of suicides, but then checked himself. Sitting here he realised he had started to circle around in the whirlpool of self-pity, which was unbecoming for a fifty-two-year-old man. Not that there was anyone who would care enough to notice (more self-pity). It made him stand up and set up the chess pieces. He played through a few of the Kasparov games and emptied his mind of work.

After almost two hours he went to bed, feeling better about the trip. After all, if he didn't go tomorrow, he didn't have anyone else to whom to give the Polly Pocket.

5

THE FOG WAS clearing, the white blanket pulling away and revealing the two planes resting outside the hangar. He was the last one to arrive, and the others were already loading material into the hold of the larger aircraft.

He saw Max standing near the entrance to the hanger swiping through an iPad intently. The thud of his bag hitting the ground echoed off the walls. Max looked up and gave him a laconic salute.

'It reminds me of the first day of school camp.' Alexander emerging from the shadows, accompanied by Vladimir.

'School camps? Sounds luxurious.'

'You see, Vladimir? This is where Mikhail tells you how he was sent to work in a salt mine outside Vladivostok on his fifth birthday.'

He had something lined up in reply ('It was actually Yakutsk.') when he saw her emerge from the rear door of the smaller aircraft. He followed her as she sashayed down the steps and out onto the tarmac. She stopped, turned around, squealed something back in reply to whoever was still in the cabin, turned back around giggling, then lit a cigarette.

He inhaled deeply to force down what he was feeling. Anger, surprisingly. What the hell was the girl doing here, surrounded by the jackals Alexander had swept up, skipping into this like it was some college vacation? He thought about the toy, wrapped up and sitting in his overnight bag.

A few seconds passed before he noticed Alexander and Vladimir standing next to him, grinning. 'You're not still thinking about her, are you?' (Alexander.) They watched as another girl emerged and sat on the stairs. 'Snatch like that will drive you batshit insane.' (Vladimir.) He turned and looked at Vladimir. Alexander clapped Vladimir on the back and told him to check with Max that they weren't waiting on anyone else.

The second girl had disappeared back inside, and Taisia was standing alone on the edge of the shadow of the hangar swiping through her phone. They were both walking towards her, and he wondered whether Alexander was accompanying him or if it was the other way round. 'Max said you had everything under control with the convoy prep.' He gave a noncommittal nod. They had reached the plane but Taisia hadn't looked up from the phone.

'We've been sitting on the damned plane for an hour, Alexander, why were we dragged here at 5:30?' Taisia said, still swiping through the phone. 'You should tell him to be careful about being around such a crazy fucking person

– I might drag him down to my dumb girl level.' He and Alexander looked at each other, one of them enjoying the scene more than the other.

He was formulating a response when Alexander stepped in on his behalf: 'Mikhail was telling me, Taisia, that he feels that you and he may have gotten off on the wrong foot the other day.' She still hadn't looked up from the phone. It was obvious (even to Mikhail) that she was pretending to still be scrolling through important information. He felt flattered at being the target of such an ostentatious attempt at conversational exclusion. Alexander again: 'Mikhail?'

'I feel like she and I got off on the wrong foot the other day,' he said. He thought (stupidly) that might have got a smile from the girl. She took a drag of her cigarette, tossed it down and ground it into the tarmac with the point of her shoe. Then she exhaled the smoke and looked up at him for several seconds.

'I think that's Taisia's version of kiss and make up.' Alexander was still grinning when he was taken away by one of the South Africans.

He hadn't actually expected to be alone with her and cleared his throat. She looked at him expectantly and tapped her foot. 'Um…' He took a step closer to her. '… Listen, I'm sorry about how our conversation ended the other day.' Blank expression. He didn't really have a plan beyond this point. 'Um… I think… you're a good person, we're friends, you know, um, we're friends.' Her expression was difficult to read. He suddenly remembered the toy. He awkwardly rummaged in his bag, before finally retrieving it from the crevice it had slipped down into.

She was looking confused. 'Um…' – why did he keep saying that like some sort of simpleton – 'I thought you could give this to your daughter. It's a Polly Pocket,' he added, stupidly. He passed it to her gingerly and waited anxiously. She turned it over slowly, like a dinosaur handling a moon rock. One of the jet engines had roared to life, and he took the opportunity to cast around the hangar as if he were searching for someone else. Max was nowhere to be seen, and Alexander was already holding court at the back corner of the floor.

Taisia cleared her throat, and he turned back to face her. He squared up and prepared for another outburst. They looked at each other. A second of reflection: he was waiting for a crazy ex-porn star's reaction to his unsolicited gift for her daughter.

Another second, and she looked down at the wrapped box. 'Thanks for the present.'

'It's been a little while since I've wrapped a present.' A small smile, a giant spike in his happiness (pathetically). It was good to have a face that couldn't register emotion.

'I have to go. Florentina is waiting for me.' There was a brief moment where they looked at each other.

He had turned away when he heard her voice.

'Wait.' She walked slowly over to him, her face bearing a curious, almost apologetic expression.

'The girl – back on the plane – she's called Florentina.' He looked over at the plane as if she were about to appear. 'I want you… need you… to watch over her in London… she's young, she's, um… well, she's just the only other woman here, you know?'

Under normal circumstances he would have refused out of hand. His role wasn't to babysit some girl. He wouldn't even know where to begin. But he looked at her eyes and they silently pleaded with him. After a few moments he nodded, and she dropped her head in what might have been a gesture of thanks. She was still holding the Polly Pocket and she lifted it up briefly and sat it back down in her other hand, and then she turned around and went back towards the plane.

Vladimir came up to him with the final log sheets to review. 'I know we're on a deadline, but I didn't want to interrupt your time with your girlfriend.' He took the log sheets without replying. 'Alexander has some things to go over with you on the flight over about the hotel stuff.'

He glanced up briefly to see the girl disappear back into the hold of the other plane. The morning sun had broken through the clouds. He thought of their conversation and, for a few minutes, he felt good.

PART 3:

MIKHAIL

LATE FRIDAY EVENING

1

HE WAS STANDING outside the entrance to the building smoking with Alexander when his cell phone began to ring.

'Help, it's Taisia, it's Taisia!'

A look flashed at Alexander, who stiffened and threw down his cigarette.

Indistinct sobbing was blaring through his handset. He put the phone on speaker and for a moment they contemplated it.

Taisia. For a second her face – laughing, confused, angry – burst into his consciousness. He thought of her emerging from the aircraft. The phone was still in his hand, facing upwards.

'*She needs help, she needs—*' Alexander's index finger extended precisely and terminated the call.

'We need to retrieve that phone.'

Alexander raised his eyebrows. Not worthy of a verbal response, and Mikhail raised his hands in surrender. 'Let's go. We'll RV with the others. We have someone at the hotel to oversee the mopping up.' The phone started to buzz again. Alexander looked down. 'Leave it, there's nothing that we can do now.' He thought back to Taisia in the café telling him her heavily abridged life story.

And then he turned to start to run.

He felt a hand on his shoulder and he faced Alexander's admonitory glare.

'Don't go.'

Sound advice. They needed to leave, just like he'd done after the crash in the Congo. Florentina called again, and with Alexander glaring at him, he answered the call. Her wailing razored through the air. In the next instant he shook himself free of Alexander's tightening grip and scrambled away.

'Call Max! *Call Max!* Tell him to activate the contingency plan – the fucking Arabs will be leaving *now*!'

He didn't hear Alexander's last words to him.

He knew that Max and his men were scheduled to bivouac in a car park near one of the ring roads, but as he heaved himself down the pavement towards the hotel he could not for the life of him remember the exact location. Whether they would have enough time to coalesce into position at such short notice was doubtful, and with each heavy step towards the hotel he could feel his professional reputation dissolving.

Alexander had turned and reached the door by the time he was running in earnest. An image of Taisia holding that goddamn Polly Pocket flashed through his mind as he accelerated. He stumbled over a crack in the pavement and his free hand slapped the ground hard and painfully.

The phone bounced along the concrete. He picked up the cracked screen and could hear even before he put it back up to his ear that she was still going.

His heart was pumping bloodied ice into his throat as he tried to rasp out a further reply to Florentina's wailing. The sobbing had increased as he rang off and tried to accelerate, tried to force his legs to move faster and faster as he tried to dodge the drunks ambling in clumps down the street.

The other phone was already vibrating in his jacket pocket as he swung round the corner and collided with a young woman on the edge of a group. She cannonballed into her friends and he was spun around.

A cacophony of outraged screams, led by a male soloist: 'Oi! Fucking hell, mate, what the fuck?!' The beat of his heart accelerated and a bulky shape was stepping quickly towards him. He reached into his pocket, pulled out his wallet and threw the wad of twenty-pound notes in their direction, and didn't wait for their reaction to the currency fluttering down into the gutter.

There was only a block to go to the hotel. The cracked phone was vibrating in his fist again and his breathing was loud and ragged. A taxi horn blared at him as he ran across the intersection as the traffic light turned green. He didn't answer the phone and kept running; each vibration of the phone felt more urgent.

Finally he rounded the corner and saw the glow of the entrance to the Mayflower hotel. A bellhop was having a furious argument with a group of Arabs on the steps. Nobody looked at him as he barrelled into the lobby.

Inside the hotel, he threaded through the oncoming wave of the drunken entourage members, laden down with suitcases and extra clothes. There was an Arab screaming into a phone in English about getting the plane ready.

He couldn't see the Prince, couldn't see Taisia or Florentina.

Nearby he recognised the Arab informant Ghalib talking discreetly on the phone in Russian. He grabbed Ghalib's arm: 'Give me your key card – I need to get up to the suite.' Here the Arab looked up at him angrily and he added, 'Alexander sent me – there should also be an ambulance arriving shortly. Quickly, quickly!' He realised he was clinging to Ghalib's arm desperately.

Ghalib wrenched his arm away and yelled in English, 'They've just cancelled all the key cards – nobody can use the elevator!' He forced down the panic. 'How much money do you have with you? ...Don't look at me like that, just get it out and come with me.'

Behind the commotion, one of the retinue had dropped one of the carry bags she was struggling with and was trying to scrape the necklaces and cartons of cigarettes off the floor; a bodyguard was stuffing wads of American dollars into his jacket pocket; the concierge was trying to block the path of another young girl with an armful of handbags; a young blonde receptionist was scurrying towards the elevator.

Ghalib had seen her first, and was closer, and he had already circumnavigated the abandoned luggage trolley. Ghalib hadn't dragged himself across half a neighbourhood while stuck on the phone. The elevator doors were opening as the Arab bounded up to the girl and grabbed her shoulder.

It took a second for him to realise what was happening at the elevator. He lunged forward and tripped over a loose high-heeled shoe and slapped the ground hard. The whirring sound of the plane tumbling to earth had returned as he tried to scrape himself off the lobby floor. One of his phones was vibrating in his pocket again.

The increasing pain in his knee made it hard to stagger to his feet. It must have been during this time that Ghalib had produced the flick knife. Mikhail barrelled over to the elevator, past an Arab girl laden with suitcases. The joints in his leg were white hot, and he was still short of breath.

He jammed his arm between the closing steel jaws. They jerked back outwards and revealed the lobby girl's tear-streaked white face. Ghalib looked at him viciously over her shoulder. 'Quickly,' he hissed. The girl was shaking and Mikhail was wheezing and his heart was still hammering. 'Let… her…' (coughing) '…go…' Ghalib gripped the girl's shoulder and she cried out in pain, and he mashed the button to close the doors. Ghalib hadn't responded, and was still holding the knife in the small of the girl's back.

Mikhail was leaning against the wall of the elevator car, trying to catch his breath. The floor was plastered with loose American dollar bills. The whirring of the plane crashing to the earth had returned. The hotel girl was looking at him pleadingly, and he felt hopeless, encased in the plush metal box. The box began to ascend. Ghalib and the hotel girl both saw him looking at the red emergency button. The girl sobbed and Ghalib smirked at him as the numbers on the digital display flipped upwards towards 33.

'It will be OK. Nobody is here for you to get hurt.' She sobbed harder as Ghalib's smirk widened and he grabbed the girl's hair hard. Her scream lasted past 27 and 28. 'Don't know why Alexander sent some broken-down geriatric here…' Ghalib spat at him. '…You should see yourself there.' (Twenty-nine, level 30.) Ghalib shoved her right up against the doors. His right hand had moved to grip the girl's shoulder and she whinnied in pain.

As he braced himself against the wall he could hear the shouting and wailing enveloping the room. He inhaled and launched himself out of the elevator. The room was strewn with overturned furniture, broken glass, discarded clothing. The hotel girl crumpled into an armchair and sobbed.

And down the end of the cavernous room, near the entrance to the bedroom, were two people hunched over a pair of legs. As Ghalib strode towards them he could make out a black African kneeling next to Florentina. He had no idea what the black man was doing there.

Ghalib was holding a knife. In the next second he realised what might have been about to happen. He realised it, but he couldn't believe it. It was brutal, reckless, insane. What had Alexander said to him? Had Alexander ordered this specifically, or was this Ghalib's terrible misinterpretation of the order?

He put the phone – the only weapon he had – to his ear and spoke at the top of his voice. '…Yes – police, police

– penthouse suite of Mayflower Hotel. An Arab – name of Ghalib – there's a dead girl and he has a gun – help, help, he's killing people! Come! Come!'

An electric current whipped through the three of them. Ghalib stopped dead. Florentina whimpered in grief and terror. The second it took for Ghalib to see through the tissue-thin ploy was enough for the black man to seize him from behind and wrap his elbow tightly around the throat. The Arab started to thrash violently, his legs splayed out as the knife fell to the floor. The two women were struck mute with white terror. Mikhail lurched forward and snatched the knife off the carpet. He hobbled across the room, past the two struggling men, to Florentina.

A gurgling sound was coming from the Arab. Florentina had begun crying, 'Tochukwu! Tochukwu!' (which he realised after a few seconds was the African's name).

'Do you know the black?' he asked the girl.

She seized his arm violently and desperately. 'Stop him! Stop him! The police will arrest him!' Her bloodshot eyes looked at him pleadingly. An angry grey and purple bruise was emerging under her eye, and the sound of the aeroplane falling to earth grew louder and louder. Behind him there was more cumulative grunting and struggling. 'Taisia's gun – it's over there, under the chair, *Tochukwu*!' Her words morphed into an anguished screech.

He turned back. Tochukwu and the Arab were exhausted. He grabbed Florentina's arm firmly. 'Get me that gun, *now*.' The girl stared back at him insensibly and he squeezed her upper arm until she squealed in pain. 'Now!' he said though gritted teeth. He wrenched her in the direction of the chair. She started to crawl, whimpering and crying like a wounded animal.

He stood up and walked over to the two men, panting and scrabbling on the floor. The Arab had turned a shade of turquoise and was still gargling and rasping away. Mikhail grabbed Tochukwu under the shoulders and dragged him away. He lay flat and unprotestingly in the middle of the hotel room, exhausted and breathing heavily. The Arab rolled onto his side and pressed his head resignedly on the carpet.

He felt a light tapping on his arm. It was the girl gingerly trying to hand him the gun. He spoke harshly – much more harshly than he had intended: 'Don't give it to me, give it to your friend. Tell him to keep an appropriate distance from the Arab. Do it now.' He heard her scurry over to Tochukwu.

He crouched down and – for only a second – gazed at Taisia's lifeless eyes staring upwards. A faint blue tint was beginning to seep into the beautiful white Barbie-doll complexion. Her mouth was slightly open in the expression of the existential dismay of the dead. The noise he was hearing had stopped and now his ears were ringing. His heart shrivelled as he thought of her silhouette sashaying into the aircraft hangar. And then Florentina's crying and wailing broke through the feedback and he snapped himself shut and turned around.

'He wouldn't give Taisia the phone! He wouldn't hand over the, the…' The end of the sentence was inaudible. He had known as soon as he got Florentina's call that Vladimir hadn't succeeded in getting the safe open. His own phone was buzzing again, and he took it out of his pocket and answered Alexander's call.

'The target has been stopped en route. Packages acquired. No casualties.'

'Taisia's dead. I'm here now in the room. The situation will be resolved. The Arab tried to kill the other girl. I know it was you who sent him. I hold you responsible for what he tried to do.' He ended the call.

He felt a delicate touch on his upper arm and he turned around. Florentina's sobbing face confronted him. She was holding a phone, a gold-plated iPhone with a cracked screen. He took if from her and nodded. He knew from the briefing material that there was at least a second phone, supposedly kept in the safe in the other room, that had the business contacts and information.

'How did you get this?' he asked stupidly.

'I saw it...' She coughed pathetically. '...I saw it when the Prince took off his coat – he put it in his jacket pocket but he was so drunk and it fell on the floor. Gold plating. So fucking stupid. I pushed it under the bed when I was on the ground and they were leaving,' she mumbled. He was about to say something to her, but she had already returned to her vigil at Taisia's side. The phone felt heavy (the gold plating was very impractical). There wasn't the time to evaluate its significance.

Ghalib was kneeling facing the bedroom wall with his hands behind his head. Florentina was bent over Taisia whispering some nonsensical incantation. He watched as she crawled over to a clutch bag resting on the carpet away from Taisia's head and extracted a Samsung phone.

'What the hell are you doing?'

She looked at the phone briefly as if to confirm something for herself, and then she scrabbled her way back to the body.

He went over, grabbed her by the arm and pulled her to her feet. She screamed in protest. 'No! We can't leave her – we can't leave her here!' She was waving the phone around wildly.

They had to leave Taisia there. Alexander would be sending someone else imminently. He grabbed her hard and actually shook her. 'We have to go now! Let me take that.' He prised the phone from her grasp and put it in his jacket pocket.

'It's Taisia's phone – it has all the photos of Lada and the, and the, and the messages… it has—'

'I have it now. It's safer with me. Let's go, we're about to be caught—'

'Tochukwu! He has to come with us.' Fucking Tochukwu. He felt a seething rage, an infuriating, unjustified exasperation for the girl and for the African. So when the Arab stabbed Tochukwu in the neck with a penknife a moment later, he really did feel bad.

An unearthly shriek was torn out of Florentina. He ran towards the Arab as the African fell to the ground, blood running out of his mouth and out of his neck. Tochukwu hit the ground and the gun went off with a startling crack. The Arab had unwisely taken a step back after plunging the knife in. His weight was too far back and he tried to hurl himself forward awkwardly towards the gun's resting place on the carpet.

It gave Mikhail time to lunge forward and scoop the gun from the floor. He grabbed it and pointed it upwards towards the ceiling as Ghalib swung forward. He fired, and then fired again, then tried to fire again. It was the second shot that went through his throat. A hideous ringing and an explosive cough of blood everywhere. His eyes widened and bulged, and then went dead, and he crumpled in a heap to the side.

Mikhail was splayed out on his front on the carpet. The ringing hadn't dissipated, but it was drowning out Florentina. He was still hyperventilating. After a minute or two (or maybe it was longer, or shorter; his mind was still scrambled) he struggled to his knees and looked around.

So.

The room was a macabre tableau. Beyond the overturned armchair and the table covered in half-empty vodka bottles, Florentina was bent in prayer over the African. A dark red shell spread across the carpet around his head. He didn't need to check whether he was still alive. The Arab's head had lolled backwards, revealing the blood trickling down from the hole in his neck and chin.

The hotel girl was cowering next to an armchair.

He went over to her. 'I'm sorry.' He crouched down so he was level with the girl's terrified face. 'What is your name?'

She didn't look at him. Eventually whispered that it was Marion.

'Marion, I want you to wait here. I will get her in a moment and we will go down in lift together. Nobody is going to hurt you. But I need you to wait with my friend.'

Well, what else was he going to call Florentina? Marion nodded slightly, but she didn't look at him. Not that he blamed her. After a pause, Marion stood up and tiptoed shakily over towards Florentina.

There was a long, smeared stain of blood on the carpet where (he assumed) Florentina had dragged Taisia in the waning seconds of her life. He went into the bedroom ensuite and looked at himself in the mirror. Blood had spattered across his face and into the crevices of his injury; by instinct he was still gripping the Beretta hard. He rinsed his face, put the safety back on the gun and placed it behind himself in his trouser waistband like he was some hood in a Hollywood movie.

A thought occurred to him and he went back across the length of the room, back past the discarded clothes, broken furniture, past the second bathroom, past a dining table covered in food and empty bottles, into the far back corner next to a walk-in closet. The room was still as he looked at the small, black box. The door was slightly ajar. He bent down and pulled it open gently and looked into the empty, colourless void.

For a moment he let his thoughts swirl as he cursed himself violently for agreeing to be part of this. He stood up, kicked the safe and listened to empty metal shudder reverberate through the air.

It would have been better for him if he had never come back to the hotel. There was no rational reason to do it. One phone call from a porn star in trouble and he had dropped everything and rushed into a disaster that shouldn't have had anything to do with him. Arrived, moreover, with no idea of what had happened, no weapon, no plan.

These were considerations even before he had killed someone.

The phone was still smouldering in his pocket. He inhaled and took it out.

Seven missed calls, five messages. four calls from Alexander, three from Max.

He looked at Max's messages:

11:47pm: Indications that convoy is on the move – do you have eyes on any of the Arabs?
12:01am: You need to evac from the hotel ASAP.
12:13am: We have seen the vehicles on the traffic cameras, are in position, get back to base NOW!
12:33am: The convoy was halted successfully. Merchandise recovered.

And, as he walked back round from the corner towards Florentina and Taisia, he looked at Alexander's only message:

12:17am: Mikhail. Don't do this – leave them and get back here. It's not worth it.

Surprisingly restrained.

He called Max back and the call was answered on the first ring. 'Max, Max, you need to stall Alexander and the rest of them. Tell him I've retrieved the phone and some other material…' He was still out of breath. '…Do everything you can to prevent them leaving without me…' He coughed, and he thought some more. '…Tell him that… otherwise… I'll make it very difficult for him.'

Max replied, 'Mikhail, I've already done more than I should. I can't do any more.' And then a dial tone.

He tried to make himself relax as he went back to retrieve Florentina and Marion. Just in time to see the elevator doors close as Marion went down to the ground floor. He pressed the elevator button desperately again and again. He turned around wildly.

Florentina had returned to Taisia's body and had dragged her torso upright and was clasping it tightly. She was wailing uncontrollably again.

Taisia was drooping forward over Florentina's shoulder: her skin had become very pale; her tongue lolled out of her mouth pathetically. For another second he was seized with a terrible grief; his whole body felt impossibly heavy and tired, as if he was being sucked into the earth.

But there was no more time for that. Each second he and Florentina stayed in the hotel room allowed Alexander more room to regroup and seal off their escape routes. Now that Mikhail had ignored the abort order, the logical next step would be to get the English police to box him and Florentina in the hotel and discreetly leave the country. Presumably it had been the original intent for Ghalib to eliminate anyone who could tie the rest of them to a crime scene and then retreat back home beyond the reach of British extradition laws.

But Alexander didn't know whether he had possession of the Prince's phone; he didn't know whether the safe had been opened, and that may still be useful. Ghalib wouldn't be returning Alexander's calls, and there would be conclusions drawn from that.

The room was silent, and he assumed Florentina was in shock. Above the elevator door was an art deco dial. He stared at it as it began to swing from G through the first few levels.

He thought he heard the wail of sirens outside and contemplated the prospect of an English prison cell. His mind wandered idly and he considered the fact that the penthouse suite, for all its extravagant luxury, didn't have any apparent access to a fire escape. In the event of emergency its guests would presumably be confined to their gilded top-floor cage as the flames rose higher. The dial had gone past '10' and was swinging slowly towards '24'.

He looked over towards Florentina, slumped pathetically over Taisia. 'The elevator is almost here!' She didn't react. He thought about leaving her behind (a moot point if the distraught Marion had alerted the authorities – whoever that might be – to the scene in the penthouse). It wouldn't be the worst thing he'd ever done. She could be detained, questioned, released, and then… Well, to ask the question was to answer it. Alexander wasn't going to let her stagger around London wailing about her dead girlfriend.

And she was so dumb. Just so fucking dumb. He reproached himself for thinking it. But he thought of her asking him about Afghanistan and her blank stare in the café. It would be like leaving an injured kitten next to a crocodile.

The elevator door opened and revealed an empty car. The room's silence felt deeper. Florentina still hadn't moved.

'Come on!' he hissed. She was there, determined to give due respects to a woman when nobody else would, whose qualities the world had refused to recognise. It was infuriating.

She had resumed whispering something to Taisia.

'*Florentina, get over here now! We have to leave now! Right now. Leave Taisia – leave her!*' She'd driven him insane. He heard the doors begin to close and he didn't know which way to turn. He stepped onto the threshold of the elevator car and the doors recoiled.

She finally lifted up her head. Her eyes were a deep blood red, and streaks of black eyeshadow flowed down her face. It was tiring just to look at her. He had trouble understanding her wail: 'I'm not leaving her! You go, but I'm… I-I-I'm staying here w-with… with Taisia!' She turned her back to him.

He was still standing on the edge of the elevator in a frozen pose when it started its plaintive buzz. Each buzz grew louder, its pitch shredding his nerves. Florentina paused her incantations and looked back towards him. 'You have to go! I can stay here, I… I… I haven't done anything wrong!'

She was sobbing again. For another second he stayed standing in the buzzing entrance. Then he thought of the hotel girl Marion spreading the news of the activities in the penthouse, and he knew he had no other choice.

Florentina was kneeling on the stained carpet, leaning

forward, her small hands resting on the ground cupped in front of her in some gesture of supplication. He bounded towards her, past the dead African. Behind him he heard the buzzing stop abruptly and the elevator's jaws slam shut. He jammed the button with his finger again and again, and in response the elevator dial swung insouciantly towards 'G'.

He imagined the car ascending back towards them, brimming with police and Marion and hotel managers. Florentina had rolled onto her back and was lying perpendicular to Taisia, staring at the ceiling. The tension left him. He thought back to his conversation with Taisia in the café. There was nothing that could be done now. He went over to an armchair (the one not lying on its side) and dropped down into it.

There was a long, long, meditative silence and then sound of the doors sliding open. And then… nothing. No police, no management, no Marion, no vengeful Arabs. And then there was only a second left to act.

He launched himself back onto his feet and lunged towards Florentina. Her slender arm was stretched wanly above her head and he seized her forearm roughly. She shrieked defiantly, 'No! No! Fuck you, *no*!' She had made her body go limp and he tried drag her across the carpet, eliciting louder screams. She took a breath and he heard the mechanical sound of the elevator doors closing again.

He leant forward, grabbed her waist and heaved her over his shoulder. Burning ice was sliding down his throat again, and he pivoted back around as she beat his back with her fists like they were in some *Popeye* cartoon. He stumbled to the door and jammed his foot in the gap. The door recoiled back and he threw himself inside the car. He lost his balance and felt his knee give way. Florentina's weight pressed down upon him and the pain in his knee intensified. He rolled his shoulder and cast her into the corner of the elevator. The girl screamed theatrically, almost comically, before coming to rest. She looked defeated.

He swivelled round and pressed '4', the gymnasium and swimming pool level. The button flashed momentarily and then faded. The doors closed, but the elevator didn't move.

'You need a key card if you want to go anywhere but the ground floor,' Florentina said dully. The unfortunate Marion flashed through his mind and he cursed himself for forgetting this obvious fact. He tried to open the doors but again: a blink, then nothing. The two were encased in the elevator car. 'We have to wait until someone on another floor orders it.' He looked back at her but checked his anger when he saw the state she was in. Florentina had closed her eyes and leant her head against the wall. The bruise on her face was turning from yellow to an angry purple.

He gave the number 4 one last angry bash. Then the silence enveloped them and he stepped back. He looked at his watch. They were at the mercy of whichever Johnny Lunchpale was staggering back to his room at 12:48am. Or the police, of course.

The elevator began to descend. A brief survey of the evidence – the two (wait, three) dead bodies, the theft of the phone, the assault of a hotel employee – obscured the fact that nobody had really done anything seriously wrong (that is, nobody who was still alive). Marion could testify to that. Perhaps. He had, after all, told Ghalib to let her go.

The descent continued. Level 6 passed by, then level 5. The girl had opened her eyes and stared ahead indifferently, her head still leaning against the mirrored glass, her lipstick smeared at an oblique red angle. The car descended past level 3 (restaurant, hair salon) and stopped at level 2 (swimming pool, gymnasium). The doors pulled apart for a squat Filipino cleaner with a vacuum strapped to her back pushing a cart. A key card was attached to a lanyard was dangling from her belt.

Florentina didn't move from the back corner of the car. He stood on the threshold blocking the cleaner from entering. The cleaner glared at him expectantly. 'Florentina, come on, this is our floor.' No reaction. The infernal shriek of the elevator resumed again, and the cleaner started to shout. He turned around and seized her arm again and yanked it towards him. She stumbled as he pulled her towards him, and her body splayed awkwardly into him. The cleaner exploded with rage after he stepped backwards to regain his balance and trod on her foot.

Excuse me! Why don't you apologise?'

He didn't apologise. They needed that key card. He realised he was staring at it like a demented pervert. The cleaner looked at him, her lined and tired face arranged in slow motion into a mask of horror.

Mikhail stepped close to her, looming over her and making his eye go dead. She shrunk back, trembling.

'Give. The key card. To me.'

Her eyes darted to Florentina and back to him. The shaking hand paused as it reached for the key card. He narrowed his eyes and breathed in, and she snatched at the key card. He clasped her hand and detached the card from the lanyard.

Then he shoved the cart further back (shrieks of horrified indignation) and started to drag Florentina down the corridor. The buzzing stopped as the cleaner pulled her cart back into the elevator. She was still chastising them both in flurried English as the doors closed on her.

Dimmed lamps were at intervals down the corridor, casting a repeating yellow glow that merged into the quiet. The girl had leant her forehead against the wall and was crying again. He realised that she wasn't wearing any footwear, and this was yet another problem to add to the list.

'Florentina.'

Surprisingly, she turned her head towards him, the good eye peering at him like she was a frightened animal.

'We have to keep moving. I know it's very hard; I know that it's the last thing in the world you feel like doing, but we can't stop.'

The eye closed and the slumped body was still for a moment. Then she breathed and shuddered and rotated her body, revealing her other eye. The bruise had spread, compressing her right eye to a small, bloodshot opening. She began to shuffle unsteadily towards him like a zombie.

'Here, lean on me, lean on me.'

They staggered together towards the sign to the pool.

She put her head on his shoulder and he found himself half dragging, half pushing her forward.

Then there was the realisation that he still wasn't sure whether he should abandon her altogether. The wrong girl had survived. Terrible thought. He shouldn't leave her, but it was a temptation. Florentina stumbled and fell down until she was level with his elbow. He grabbed her under her shoulder and yanked her back to her feet. She whimpered.

The two of them clumped towards the swimming pool; as she put her head back on his shoulder he tried to twist around to look back at the elevator door. He imagined the simmering cauldron the lobby had become now that another wronged and distressed employee had been dispatched down the elevator. His heartbeat began to skitter as he tried to estimate how long he had before the cleaner's key card was cancelled. Not long.

Finally they reached the entrance to the pool. Florentina had closed her eyes and let her head fall limply onto her right shoulder. He swiped the key card and there was a split second before the green light appeared. He pressed his shoulder to the door and shoved it open; the scent of chlorine assaulted them and they tripped forward onto the pool deck. As he fell he thrust his left hand out in front of him and it again slapped painfully on the ground. Florentina collapsed on top of him and then rolled over onto the ground.

The lapping of the water echoed around the room. Once again he heaved himself to his feet. The shimmering turquoise of the pool stretched into the low fluorescent backlights of the changing-room entrances. On the ceiling the water's reflection danced to and fro. He caught his own darkened reflection in the frosted window. The right side – the normal side – was shrouded by the darkness, and the melted skin and dead eye scowled at him.

To the right of the changing rooms there was a balcony area with deck chairs and umbrellas, dimly illuminated by the glow of street signs and the backlights.

The girl had sat up and she had bent forward to rest her head on her thighs.

'OK…' – he realised how tired he now felt – 'the balcony there, that's our next destination. We're only two floors up, we should be able to find a way to climb down.' He took a look around the silent room. 'It's lucky it's so late… the cleaner might still be trying to find someone.' Optimistic, he knew.

'It's all my fault.' She hadn't lifted her head. 'It's all my fault that they're dead.' It took a few seconds to realise she was talking about the African as well. He caught his exasperation – the balcony, and escape out of the building, was so, tantalisingly close.

But one sympathised.

'And… and… I left Taisia's phone behind, with all her pictures of Lada and all because of that fucking Prince, and, and those fucking *bastards* heard me calling and they just…' She trailed off.

He went over to her and knelt down so he was level with her. She was staring into the water and more tears were rolling down her cheeks. He sighed, and he started to speak, but then he stopped himself. For a long moment they both looked blankly at the rolling surface of the pool.

Taisia had brought him here. Well, more accurately, Alexander, working through his representative here on Earth, Taisia. Right now he could have been – should have been – sitting alone in his apartment playing through a Fischer game or assembling a model. (He had to admit now that Alexander was right – he did have the same hobbies as a ten-year-old boy.) Exactly the sort of weak and useless thinking that should have been beaten out of him in Afghanistan.

His phone started ringing. It was Max, and he answered on speaker.

'Mikhail, the police are closing in. Alexander says to rendezvous near Grosvenor Square if you can. I'll message you the co-ordinates. We have… uh, we have some transport to one of the airfields. Can you confirm you have the Prince's phone? Sources suggest you have it. Mikhail? Mik—'

He ended the call. For a brief second he considered taking out the SIM card and destroying his phone. Unnecessary course of action. The phone was encrypted and – unless a miracle occurred – they were still caught in a chlorinated vice.

Florentina had stood up. He took a step towards her and froze; he felt a hammer thud in his chest. The Prince's phone. He hadn't turned it off when Taisia handed it to him. If the swimming pool had Wi-Fi it would be possible for the Prince to have wiped the phone remotely. He fumbled with the left inside pocket of his jacket, withdrew the phone, rotated it in his hand and looked at the screen.

The phone was not connected to the Wi-Fi network. There were no missed calls – he would have been alerted to them, surely? How long had it been since Taisia was killed? Forty minutes? Forty-five minutes? As he turned it off, he thought of the Prince and his entourage fleeing in a blind panic through the lobby and frantically trying to escape England. Unusual to leave somewhere without retrieving your phone; but the presence of a dead body can cloud a person's judgment.

'So are we going?

Florentina's subdued voice reached him as he was beginning to turn over a new strategy in his mind. It might work – if they could successfully reach ground level. He turned back towards her and then he looked back down at the Prince's phone. He prised open the phone and removed the SIM card. He held it between his thumb and forefinger and looked at it in the light.

Mikhail looked back at her. 'Are you wearing a bra?'

'What, are you some sort of damn pervert now?'

OK, that was his fault for not introducing this idea adequately. 'This is the SIM card from the Prince's phone. I want you to take it and put it inside your bra and I'm going to put my SIM card in the Prince's phone.'

Well, it might her keep her alive a little longer. He held out the SIM card and she eventually took it sullenly and tucked it inside her dress.

'I'm sorry if that's uncomfortable.' She didn't reply.

He inserted his own SIM into the Prince's phone and re-started it. He paused before he changed the language to Arabic. If it became necessary to bargain for her life (or his own) the ruse – however thin – might give him some small amount of leverage.

'Let's get out of here. Like I said, we need to climb down from the balcony. Now, wait here while I go and see if that will even be possible.' The girl sat down sullenly by the edge of the pool and stared glumly at the water. Her face was bathed in the aquamarine glow from the pool.

He went out onto the balcony and looked over the railing to the street below. The temperature had dropped and an icy breeze was blowing. It was immediately obvious that there was no possibility of climbing down the sheer brick wall twenty metres to the road below. He rested on the railing for a moment and laughed inwardly at the tragic absurdity of the situation he had put himself in.

The street below was quiet as he turned his phone conversations with Alexander in his mind. A few scattered couples scurried alongside the road like beetles. He thought about Taisia and Florentina and Alexander. It would have been better, all things considered, if he had declined the meeting with Taisia. He thought of her arguing on the phone outside the restaurant, and then her glassy, lifeless, doll-like eyes staring up at the penthouse roof.

A car emerged from a garage underneath a building further down the road, and turned slowly into the street. There were still sirens blaring in the distance; he couldn't tell whether they were getting louder or fainter. He placed both hands on the cold metal railing and closed his eyes for a few seconds. He hadn't considered the car park. In any event the cleaner would have made it difficult to get past the lobby. The wind whipped across the balcony as he tried to tabulate the possibilities. Looking back through the glass door he could see the outline of Florentina's torso splayed out beside the water.

As he turned to go back inside he thought back to Alexander's late-night visit and, of all things, to Gagarin and Komarov.

Everyone from his generation (but probably not Florentina's generation) knew the story. Komarov agrees to pilot the space capsule Soyuz 1 (which he knows is riddled with technical and structural problems). Were he to refuse, the mission would nevertheless proceed and his friend Gagarin would be sent in his place. Komarov undertakes the mission and the parachutes fail to open upon re-entry, sending him plummeting to Earth, cursing Brezhnev, Russia and life itself. Actually insisted beforehand that his funeral be open casket (a wish that, improbably, was honoured by the leadership). Gagarin dies in a plane crash almost exactly a year later.

The wind was still biting, and he turned and went back through the door to be enveloped by the tropical humidity of the pool enclosure. Florentina was still lying on her back staring up at the roof. The door closed behind him slowly and the pneumatic press of the latch clicking into place reverberated around the room.

'OK, change of plan,' he announced, to no reaction.

'She came back to help me.' She sobbed again, but it was cut short by a choking cough. '…It's my fault… Leave me. Just get the fuck away and leave me here.' Florentina rolled onto her side away from the water. Not exactly the stoicism of Komarov.

He turned back and forth once again in exasperation, feeling like a cheap jack-in-the-box. Two strides and he was beside her, and again he bent down and seized her underneath her thin pale arm. He tried to drag her upright once again, but his strength was still depleted. The girl made a mewling, strained sound, and her dead weight wrenched the sharp pain through joints of his shoulder and down to his elbow, and he released her back to the ground with a thud.

For a moment he stood breathing heavily (again). Ghalib had been right; he really was broken down. The thought made him furious, and he looked back down at the girl sitting there obstinately. They didn't have time to sulk, or to wallow like you were the only humans who had ever known sadness; it was so self-indulgent, so… His right hand was flat, and his forearm was tense and poised to strike; he knelt down, grabbed her, stared hardly at her and…

A pale, haggard imitation of a young woman. Her skin was cold, clammy, the purple bruise radiating further outward, and her body rattled at intervals. She looked at his hand, tensed and bowed her head into her chest in fright. He let the tension go out of his arm and then he dropped it to his side. For a moment he breathed in and out, listening to water swirling in the pool.

'Listen…' She was gazing weakly somewhere into the distance. '…Florentina, listen, we have to keep going… you have to keep going.' Florentina's gaze rolled slowly, blankly, over him and fell upon the dull light shimmering on the surface of the water.

'Florentina, Florentina, look at me.' The shock had

deepened and she was shaking. Colour drained, teeth chattering; he took both her hands and she returned the grip weakly. 'Taisia…' The words caught in his throat. '…Taisia has a daughter. She's… she's your responsibility now, you understand?'

Her eyes ranged slowly across his face, the left eye squinting at him through the greyed and blackened eyelid.

She stopped moving her head and looked at him directly. 'I need my purse. I need it, I have to go back and get it. It has my passport in it.' She made no effort to move after making this declaration. She was still gripping his hand very loosely.

He bit his lower lip and breathed in as he clenched his fists. Her eyes rolled down to his hands and then rolled back to look through him.

'How the hell could you leave your passport behind?' He regretted it the instant he said it. She snatched her hand away and narrowed her good eye.

'I'm sorry…' her voice gained strength and venom as she spoke through clenched teeth, 'if I was distracted by my f-f-friends dy…' She let out gasping cry and couldn't complete the sentence.

'Alright, alright.' He looked back towards the corridor leading to the elevator in dismay. An image appeared in his mind: a buoy bobbing aimlessly in a raging turquoise sea, rising up and sliding down mountainous waves. Leaving her passport behind would severely narrow the possibilities for returning Florentina home without incident. Without further incident. Every second that ticked by felt like a laceration.

'Where's the purse? Tell me exactly where you left it.'

She looked blank as the cogs turned slowly in her head. It took physical effort not to try to shake the information free from her. Her head slowly tilted to the right.

'I put it down. In the bedroom.' Her face was contorted in an expression of fevered concentration. 'There was a small table next to an armchair.' She looked back at him; a slight colouring had returned to her cheeks as she seized upon the recollection.

'What colour is the purse?'

'Pink. It's Furla. Well, a knock-off Furla.' A small shrug, as is she were apologising to him for this.

'I want you to stay right here. If I'm not—'

'I'm coming with you – I want to s-s-see her…'

His stomach was already constricting as he contemplated returning to the scene of a murder. He rounded on her angrily, grabbing her arm and spitting his words through tightly clenched teeth: 'You're going to stay right here until I return. There's nothing you can do for her in that room, you understand? Tell me that you understand!'

She shrunk back again like a wounded animal. There was a long moment in which they looked at each other whilst the waves lapped.

'OK.' Her voice was barely a whisper. A small mercy.

'If I don't return in ten minutes…' Her glassy expression had returned and he felt like he was speaking a foreign language. '…Hey! Hey! You listening to me?' A slight refocusing of her eyes, but no response. He squeezed her arm until she whimpered in pain.

'You're hurting me, asshole!'

He drew her very close, so that their faces were inches apart. 'If I don't return in ten minutes, I want you to go to the lobby, ask the staff to call the police. When the police arrive, tell them you want to claim asylum in this country. Tell them that you are in fear for your life and you need to claim asylum.'

'I don't want to stay in this country. I just want to go home.'

'Just stay here.' He wasn't going to remonstrate with her any further. He turned around and strode to the elevator. The truth was he had no idea whether she would be eligible to claim asylum. Probably not. To claim asylum you had to, at a minimum, be aware that you were actually in some sort of danger, a fact that he had just failed to impress upon her.

He pressed the button and he started to hear the screeching sound of the plane crashing down to Earth. The quiet bell of the car arriving. The doors opening to an empty box. As the doors closed he could see the reflection of the water rippling on the roof and perhaps (or maybe not) the small shadow of Florentina.

As he once again ascended to the penthouse level, the volume of the screech went up and up and up. His breathing become shallow, rapid; the ice in his throat returned. The upward motion ceased. He balled his fists like he had shown Florentina and tried to regulate his breathing, sucking in the air slowly and shaking as he breathed back out and the doors opened.

The familiar, horrible chaos of the suite again. No

police, but three hotel employees – two men and a woman, huddled together speaking in hushed, urgent voices. The three bodies lay undisturbed. The shells of blood radiated out from Tochukwu and from Ghalib. And in the distance, just in front of the entrance to the bedroom, the outline of her diminutive body lying flat where he had left it. He had to take the initiative. He stepped forward into the room and let out an anguished, painful cry of despair.

'Sir! *Sir!*' The woman – late middle-aged, clearly a senior employee – broke away from the others and started to march towards him imperiously. 'Sir, I'm sorry, you can't be here, this is a crime scene!' He surged forward back across the sea of broken glass, upturned furniture and dead bodies.

He spoke in Russian: 'Taisia, Taisia! What the hell have you done?!' The woman made to put a hand out to stop him, but as he came closer she registered his face and she recoiled and jerked her hand back into her body with such force – as if she had just touched a hot stove. Whether it was the burns or the anguish he didn't know. The two men were very young – neither could have been older than twenty – and stood gormless and ineffectual behind her.

He raged at the universe as he stormed past them: 'Fuck it! Fuck it all. Why didn't you just listen to me? *Why?!*' The two men averted their eyes and turned half away; one of them made and re-made a steeple with his hands nervously. He reached Taisia. The blue colouring of her lips had spread and deepened, her body looked slighter and, most terribly, her eyes still stared up at the ceiling, completely indifferent to him, or anybody else.

'Sir…'

The voice was smaller, more diffident. He covered his face with his hands in a pose of crying. He knelt down next to Taisia. Another despairing howl. It was embarrassing, frankly.

'Sir, I'm going to have to ask you to come with me. We need you to wait downstairs in our office for the police to come.'

He had to get into that damned bedroom. He rubbed his eyes hard to make them red and he looked up at the hotel staff.

'Sir, I'm so sorry, um… you'll have to come with me.'

He held up two fingers and heaved himself up to his feet; pain shot through his knee and he stumbled forward as it almost gave way beneath him. 'Please forgive me…' – an exaggerated politeness – 'can you allow me two minutes in private? My emotion…' He looked briefly down at Taisia, lying there forlornly with all the rest of the Prince's discarded trash. He felt the sting of a tear in his eye. It was fortuitous. 'Just, please – I just need…' A catch in his throat. The woman nodded sympathetically and after a moment she bowed her head in respect and turned back towards her useless underlings.

He crossed the threshold into the Prince's erstwhile bedroom. The silent space was suffused with the amber glow from a single lamp. With the fingers on his left hand he pushed the door closed behind him very gently. He had been here not twenty minutes earlier, but it felt transposed from a terrible, ethereal nightmare – the sort that dissolved as soon as you tried to fix your mind upon it. The bedclothes were rumpled but nevertheless retained a semblance of the afternoon's visit from housekeeping.

The purse – the pink, knock-off Furla purse – lay on its side on a plush green armchair in the right corner of the bedroom. He stepped over, picked up the purse and took out the passport, then opened it and looked at the information page:

Surname: Mishkin
Name: Florentina Nikiforovich
Date of Birth: 22 March 1999
Nationality: Russian
Issued: 14 December 2018
Expiry: 14 December 2028

Florentina stared out of the page. The smallest curve of excitement on her lips broke through the standard passport page. He thought of the contrast with the person sitting despondently beside the pool downstairs. He closed the passport and tucked it inside his jacket pocket. The rest of the purse had the cheap phone he had given her, a few credit cards, perfume, tampons, lipstick. A photo of Florentina and her mother (same eyes and the cheekbones) clasped together and laughing. He took the phone and the credit cards, putting them in his outer jacket pocket.

Beyond the bedroom door he could her murmuring. He took a moment to steel himself for the journey back through the suite and to the elevator. He opened the door, saw the hotel staff in his peripheral vision and glanced sideways to verify there was not yet any law enforcement present. He knelt down by Taisia for the last time. He closed his eyes and made the sign of the cross – more an admission of his exhausted options than anything else.

The he rose to his feet and strode quickly to the elevator, looking straight ahead as he went past the woman and the gormless boy (the other having vanished). They called out to him, but he didn't take his eyes from the elevator doors as he again navigated around the party debris. He pressed the button and once again waited for police to disgorge themselves from the arriving elevator car.

As he watched the dial spin slowly towards '12' he felt them shuffle up behind him in the moment before the doors opened. A black distorted shape was reflected in the gold brass doors. He didn't turn around. A terrible hush in the final seconds and then the muffled bell of the elevator. The heavy jaws pulled apart slowly. An older man, with grey, thinning hair – his eyes ranged beyond them into the suite and surveyed it with a hard, concentrated stare.

'Jasmine, you… what are you still doing here? The police are on their way; you're not going to anyone any favours by remaining here. Come. Sir…' He was beckoning to Mikhail, but his gaze was still fixed in the distance. Jasmine and the bellhop were crossing the threshold of the car. '…Please, you must come with us and wait for the police.'

Jasmine whispered in his ear and he looked at Mikhail properly for the first time. For the merest second he was taken aback, before his professionalism re-asserted itself.

'Sir, I'm Jonathan. Jonathan Slater. I'm the night manager here. You've suffered a major shock. Please, let us help you; we can make you comfortable downstairs… if there's someone you need to contact… we can arrange some assistance for you.' Slater extended his hand from inside the elevator car.

The gun was still on his person. The logical thing, the obvious thing, would be to force the three hotel staff back into the suite at gunpoint and take the elevator by himself. The thought of Florentina slumped by the poolside waiting for his return gnawed at him. But then he looked at Slater – serious but calm, authoritative, mindful of his employees – his outstretched arm completely steady.

He ignored Slater's hand and stepped inside the elevator. The elevator had already begun to descend before he remembered to press the button for level 2. He jabbed at it repeatedly in frustration at himself. He turned to face his fellow passengers and scowled. Jasmine had taken a step back into the corner of the car, her eyes widening as she examined him up close. Slater took her arm and stared ahead at the doors; the two young men were determinedly examining the floor. The car descended. The old, habitual awareness of bystanders doing their utmost not to notice him or to make eye contact. The shared silence was heavy, the smooth, low metallic hum of the descent intensifying. He was very tired; his vision was blurred and constricted. He closed his eyes for the second that preceded the bell. A flash of anger and grief and fear and confusion. And then the doors opened, and he stepped out of the elevator and turned around.

He pressed and held the down button and looked at the three staff. 'There's another girl – waiting in the swimming pool. People will try to hurt her if she can't go home. Make sure the police don't find her.' He released the button and the doors slid closed.

He walked quickly back into the tropical humidity of the swimming pool. Florentina was sitting on the edge of the water; her knees were tucked into her body. As the door closed behind him she rotated her head and looked at him. He took out the passport and held it up for a second before replacing it in his pocked.

'We have to go. We don't have much time.'

'She told me about you.' Her mouth had curved up in a strange little smile. 'She told you me about how you gave her the toy for Lada, gave her a Polly Pocket…'

He felt a constriction in his chest as he pushed Taisia out of his mind again. 'Come, we have to move…'

She rolled her head slowly until it rested on her left shoulder. 'On the flight over… we t-t-talked about you.'

He took a step to her until he towered over the slight, shaking body. The seconds were flowing by as the police and hotel staff swarmed beneath them and Alexander marshalled his resources.

Taisia's unblinking eyes flashed through his mind again as he pulled Florentina upward and hissed at her viciously. 'I don't fucking care what she said about me. She's dead.' Florentina flinched. 'Now, if you want to leave this hotel, this country, alive…' His teeth clenched until they hurt. '…Now you are going to get on your feet, and we are getting that elevator down to the car park or so help me…' About to invoke God and fire and brimstone. It was becoming hard to tell who the insensible one was here. The water kept slapping against the sides of the pool.

Florentina had shrunk in his grip, her body hunched and tight, the skin pale and paler. Her eyes lacked focus, and her head rotated spastically to and fro.

'Let me carry you. Just to the elevator.'

She turned her head and looked at him uncomprehendingly. 'I'm relaxing with her in the house by the lake.' The childish smile returned and she didn't elaborate. Her eyeballs rotated away from him. She extended her arms behind her and leant back, extending a leg out and placing it gently on the surface of the water, and then retracting it.

'I'm going to pick you up. Understand?' No further response.

He inhaled and then knelt down on his right knee, feeling the searing pain return. 'OK, you ready?' She looked at him with mild, expectant interest, and extended her arm upon request. He pulled her forward and she flopped over his shoulder. Slowly, painfully, he rose up. His legs shook and burned as he staggered out of the pool area and then finally stumbled into the elevator door. He collapsed to the floor and she rolled off him onto the floor. Rasping on his knees, he coughed an order to the girl: 'Press the… press… the button.' More rasping. 'Florentina… please.' Finally she stood up, and in the far corner of his eye she pressed the down button and then leant her head heavily against the wall, resuming her tears. Neither of them – the bruised, beaten facsimile of a young woman and the exhausted, disfigured husk – were presentable. On the other hand, they would not immediately strike anybody as spies, thieves or murder suspects. Thieves, perhaps.

He had pulled himself to his feet again when the elevator doors opened. He had a vision of a rendezvous with the Filipino cleaner or with the team of paramedics and police shepherding the body bags on gurneys down to the ambulance and onward to the morgue. The doors slid open. A young white man in a crumbled blue suit, twirling a packet of Malboros nervously, startled when he shoved Florentina, pale and wretched, into the elevator. He stepped into the car and looked at the man viciously as the doors closed.

'Jesus, fuck.' The Marlboro man averted his eyes and took a step back against the wall. He grabbed Florentina's upper arm and dragged her next to him, and she let her head fall back onto his right shoulder. He manoeuvred her around awkwardly so he could reach over to press the button to the car park. The elevator began its descent, lowering the two of them and the Marlboro man into Hades.

There was silence as the car began its descent and the momentary disorientation of an elevator beginning to move. He dimly recalled reading about this once – Newton's laws of motion (one of them, anyway). Florentina was still slumped against him. He didn't feel comfortable, but he didn't say anything.

The elevator stopped and he balled his fists tightly and opened them again. The girl didn't move; her head dug deeply into his shoulder – advantageous, as it shielded the black eye from the public.

The quiet ding sounded as they reached the lobby. He turned away back towards the doors as they opened. There were police. Hyper-yellow jackets in the distance standing at reception. The Marlboro man exited, shaking his head in disbelief and disapproval.

He pushed the girl away and jabbed the button to close the doors again and again. As they descended once again Mikhail thought about the window of time that had elapsed and tried to piece together a hypothesis explaining what had happened:

Marion escapes down to the lobby in shock. She doesn't tell anyone else – for whatever reason – at least not immediately. Maybe it's the shock, maybe she hates her boss, maybe she was grateful to him and to Florentina for their attempts to help and wanted to give them a head start. Perhaps. She calls in the crime a little later when she's composed herself. The call is received by some receptionist flunky and may or may not be clear on the details and then there's the usual low-level organisational inertia and confusion whenever a major crime occurs on someone's shift. Then there's the delay while the police respond.

The descent came to an end and the doors opened to reveal the silent grey of the parking garage. Florentina was pressed against the side of the elevator. He grabbed her and shoved her out as the echo of a car driving over an exit hump dissipated. He grabbed her around the waist and steadied her. She was still pale and cold and shaking, and he immediately regretted handling her so roughly.

'I don't want to be here anymore,' she slurred. '…Just want to go home.'

'OK, it's OK, let's just take it slow. We're almost there.'

'Almost where?' would have been the obvious rejoinder, but she didn't say anything, just lilted back against his body. Together they shuffled like a drunken crab towards the dark of the garage exit. Inside he felt an unfamiliar emptiness. Again and again he went back to her babbling in the café and then lying dead on the Prince's room.

They got past the boom gate and were starting up the asphalt slope when Florentina tripped over her feet and fell forward. He snatched at her arm as it slipped from his grip. Her knee buckled and her left hand scraped the concrete as she fell. Screams of pain echoed around the garage. He tried to drag her upright again, but she wrenched her arm away and he saw that her hand was torn and bleeding.

'Ow, ow, ow, no!' He took her hand as delicately as he could, but she still winced and cried. She snatched it back and stayed on the ground. 'It's hopeless, everything's fucking… I don't want to be here…'

Not this again.

'…Take me back to Taisia… I should be there with her. Take me back, Mikhail. You should have taken me back up there with you!'

He swore that he could hear sirens shearing through the quiet. 'It's not too far now. Take out your phone…' He was still hurting from the running and the dragging and the fighting. '…Call a taxi. We'll go to the airport… get the hell out of this country.'

'Mikhail, Mikhail… we've just left her lying there! *They* – those fucking heartless bastards – they just left her lying there! Just left, like cowards!' She trailed off into a whimper of pain.

He didn't answer.

Florentina looked up at him pleadingly. Another black tear streaked down her desperate face. He knelt down so he was level with her. 'We can't go back. You know we can't go back. I came here to help her… I shouldn't even be here.'

She was still kneeling on the ground, and she grabbed and tugged at the front of his shirt like a kindergartener. 'We have to go back and take her with us.' He didn't know why this had resurfaced. Back at the pool he had considered striking her back to her senses and he thought back to this; the guilt clawed his insides.

Even from the relative shelter of the car park the bite of the wind could be felt. Florentina was shaking with cold and her bare arms were shrunken and thin. Through some crazed moral accounting he took off his coat and put it around her as penance for wanting to slap her. It really was cold, and by instinct he shrugged his shoulders inward and clamped his arms against his sides.

She encircled his forearm (unexpectedly) and they inched up the slope of the exit. He started to feel the painful ice return to his throat and chest.

As they shuffled he spoke. 'If they find us…' (when they find us) 'the others, I mean. Remember what I taught you. Ball your fists, regulate your breathing… keep close to me…' he coughed, 'and whatever you do, whatever you do, don't mention the goddamn phone.'

They reached the street, and they stopped. Quiet. A few scattered people were walking down the street. No police. Yet. He scanned the area for a cab. If they could get a ride to Gatwick, he could place her separately on a commercial flight home and then make contact with Alexander to smooth things over.

'OK, I—'

'Be honest with me...' She looked at him and lips were trembling. '...Do I look... do I look... ugly right now?' Her face was backlit by the fluorescent lights from the parking garage. The blue-green bruise had intensified further, and the streaks of eyeliner and makeup criss-crossed her cheeks. He paused too long and her face collapsed.

'Listen...' He didn't know what he was going to say, but it didn't matter because the van appeared and the ex-Spetsnaz guys bundled them both inside.

PART 4:

MIKHAIL

1

THE TWO EX-SPETSNAZ stared at them both as the van pulled away. Florentina had leant her head upon the window. The one on the left looked like concrete poured and set into a jumpsuit. He had no visible neck, and his shaved head was almost a cube. The man looked like a human cinderblock. The one on the right wore a tracksuit, his features facial features compressed like a bulldog, a nose that had healed imperfectly after being broken too many times.

'You both look like shit,' said the Cinderblock.

Neither Mikhail nor Florentina looked at them. Mikhail was trying to figure out how they had been found so quickly. Which was a waste of time and energy in any event (Alexander had probably just assigned someone to watch each egress point – but he didn't have the manpower spare to do that, surely?). He also wondered where Alexander was.

As it turned out, he didn't have to wait long for an answer to both these questions. Florentina was staring at her phone. 'Alexander is already at the airport hangar in Hampshire, wherever that is. I thought we came in somewhere different,' Florentina mumbled.

'How do you know?'

'I can see him on Find My Friends. He might have forgotten that we added each other a few weeks ago. Most people forget they have still have it working.'

He turned to face her, couldn't find the words and then turned back. The Bulldog and the Cinderblock were smirking at him.

Cinderblock: 'She's a real Nobel prize winner, this one.' The Bulldog just grinned like a lump of human play-doh. Mikhail let his head fall back in his seat.

They turned through an intersection and onto a major road (he should have been able to name it, but again nothing turned upon it any longer). He turned his head slowly to the right to keep the blurred shape of the girl in his peripheral vision.

They hadn't patted them down and Taisia's gun was still in his waistband. The driver hadn't turned around, but he thought he recognised him as one of the men that Max had sourced. A few silent minutes passed and they had moved beyond the centre of the city and onto a ring road. Bars of fluorescence pierced the dark of the cabin as they passed through the streetlights.

The human Cinderblock and the Bulldog both looked bored; their eyes were so blank he swore he could see through into their empty, cavernous skulls. As the van accelerated further he laid back and weighed the merits and the demerits of shooting the driver in the head. In his imagination he watched the driver slumping over the wheel, the passengers being thrown violently sideways and Florentina bouncing back and forth like a rag doll.

Difficult to see how this would confer a strategic advantage.

Florentina was in tears again. The Bulldog and the Cinderblock looked uncomfortable as she dug her head into the seat and vibrated with sorrow. He thought about reaching out to take her hand gently (in doing the rounds with grieving families after Afghanistan, this had been his best – indeed, his only – move). But now was perhaps not the time for sentimentality.

The journey continued in silence, as they began to roll through the industrial outskirts of the city. Warehouses and square concrete buildings appeared fleetingly as grey smudges beyond the freeway. At one point the Bulldog looked at him, and he stared back at him without emotion until he turned back away.

Eventually the van reached the airfield. It was now almost 3:00am. The van slowed to allow the infrared sensors to read the licence plate and the boom gate lifted upwards in a slow, controlled arc. They skated over the smooth tarmac towards the hangar, which glowed yellow against the dark electric blue of the night sky.

Florentina stirred slowly as they stopped outside the hangar. Two light planes (Beechcrafts?) were being readied.

The driver and the Bulldog exited, and Mikhail unbuckled his seatbelt. Florentina didn't move.

'Out,' the Cinderblock grunted.

He reached out quickly and shook her before somebody else did it. 'Come on, quickly, stick close to me. Quickly!' She complied mechanically, opening her door and almost falling out onto the ground. He was alert now, even more so than he had been back at the hotel, and he leapt out his side, went round and took her arm.

She leant against him pathetically like she had in the parking garage.

'Stand up. Stand up straight!' he commanded.

The girl tried to comply and rose unsteadily to her full height. 'I just want to go home. Can you do that? Just let me go home.'

He looked down at the sickly and tired doll, and she looked back indifferently. 'Now take my arm. Take it!' She grabbed his arm weakly.

'Hurry up. Get the fuck inside. Leave her here with us.' Then one of the play-doh men shoved him hard and he dragged her with him through to the hangar, footsteps echoing behind them.

'Leave her. Mikhail is her knight in shining armour. After all, nobody else will take her.' Alexander's voice echoed from above. Mikhail's eye took in the hangar – the two planes, the men disassembling the weapons, an Arab's body being zipped into a body bag – before he finally looked up.

A raised metallic catwalk ran down the side of the hangar. Alexander looked down impassively.

Florentina loosened her grip suddenly, lunged forward and dropped to her knees. 'Alexander, Alexander, you have to help! …We left Taisia behind at the hotel… We have to go back for her! You love her like I do… We have to… we have to go now!' She uttered a cry and then bent forward until her forehead almost touched the smooth black surface.

Alexander placed both his hands on the railing and leant forward slightly. He tilted his head to the right, looked at her with a detached curiosity like she was a crushed beetle clinging on to life. Mikhail looked from Alexander down to Florentina and then back again.

'Alexander, I have to get her on a separate plane. There's no use in keeping her around us. She's just—'

Alexander cut him off, his voice scything through the air. 'The question is, "Why?"' He had fixed Mikhail with an immovable glare. The final word cracked like a whip. 'Why you – *you* – of all people, did this! And for what? For what?'

The girl lay prostrate on the floor of the hangar, whimpering. A barely audible squeak emerged from the small body. 'He came to help her… He didn't know… he didn't know she was… that… shewasdead!' The final three words were forced out in one slurred sound. Neither man moved. In the distance the men were reaching the final stages of loading the various cargo onto the planes.

'Taisia. Poor Taisia.'

Less a eulogy than a recitation of a mundane fact, like pi to four decimal places or the capital of Azerbaijan.

'We recovered a number of useful things from the Prince and his confreres. But…' Alexander let the words ripple through the room before continuing, 'but there was no weapon. A lot of money. Some documents. Everyone will have to get the coke dry cleaned out of their clothes. But no gun. And no phone.'

One of the men grabbed him from behind and ripped off his jacket. Mikhail stared ahead as the phone and gun was slid across the hangar floor. 'I need to put the girl on a separate plane back home. Otherwise…' He paused. Dramatic effect. '…The job will remain unfinished.'

Alexander didn't react. Florentina remained on her knees, head bowed forward until it touched the ground, like she was an Egyptian slave in the presence of the pharaoh.

'Alexander, the planes are almost ready. We're monitoring the police chatter back at the hotel. There's not much time left.'

A young man he didn't recognise had appeared next to Alexander. He wore a smart, tailored jacket; stylish haircut; eyes narrowed and black; and his mouth shrivelled in a look of disdain.

Florentina was looking upwards to the catwalk. She dragged herself to her feet with another piercing, tortured scream like a banshee being raised from the dead. Everyone stopped what they were doing and stared.

'*You, you!*' The girl was drained completely of colour, her eyes were sunken and furious, and she started towards the new man on the catwalk. Her neck was craned back and she kept the man fixed with a murderous glare as she stumbled forwards. Mikhail grabbed her as she barrelled past and her arms flailed outwards as he pulled her back to him.

'I saw you! I saw you! You were running. You saw her dying and you just ran!' Her voice rose and subsided and rose again. 'You left her to die! You fucking... coward! You... you...' The girl seized his arm with both hands and whimpered. Her body was clammy and she somehow felt as if she had shrunk since the hotel; her body felt no heavier than a child.

'Sergei. Or whatever your fucking name is...' She was clutching his arm as if he were a buoy in a raging sea. '...You're no better than a murderer. You're trash, you're going to burn in hell. She's a mother, and you left her to die like she was nothing!'

Sergei flinched and his eyes flicked to Alexander, and then to Mikhail. Mikhail looked through him. Florentina was right. He was nothing, so he wouldn't waste a display of emotion on a man who was nothing.

Sergei spat over the railing. 'Fuck you, fuck you, fuck your stupid whore there with a room-temp IQ, and fuck that dead bitch. A tragic loss to the next Cumsluts 14 upload for Pornhub.' Mikhail looked at Florentina, but she didn't move or respond. Sergei, in full flight of injured innocence, was actually hyperventilating.

Alexander remained immobile.

Florentina wasn't finished. She broke free of his grip and lunged forward, but she tripped and fell to her knees. Mikhail took a step forward and tried to lift her back up to her feet, but she sank back down like a stone.

'You're pathetic. You weren't fit to be in the same room as her, you piece of...'

Mikhail heaved her back up to her feet and she tried to lunge forward again; he pulled her back. She whiplashed into him, her body slight and limp like a rag doll. He looked back up at Alexander. The catwalk was now almost directly above him, and he craned his neck back and rolled his eyes upwards. One of the large circular halogen lights framed Alexander's head so that he appeared as a blank silhouette, with only the barest outline of the nose and his left eye visible. An unmoving, emotionless shadow staring down from above.

Taisia intruded back into his thoughts and he hated himself all over again for his grief. Sergei had been placed there by Alexander to taunt him, to break him down.

He looked at the girl who was now stuck to him like a limpet. And then he looked back upwards to the two blank silhouettes. He thought things over. He looked over at the others loading the last of the materiel onto the planes.

Sergei was laughing and began to speak but was cut off by Alexander. '…Get down there and finish the damn pack. Pick up that phone. You've said your piece.'

Sergei smirked as he began to slowly stomp down the catwalk stairs to the floor; the metallic clang smote the air over and over again.

'Tell me something I can't work, out Mikhail…' He was still a dark smudge against the blinding light. '…Maybe I'm missing something, maybe I'm just not that smart. Now, we get the call in from your friend here. You blast out of the starting blocks like it's the gold-medal event at the geriatric games. Riding into the hotel on your white horse to save the day. Some porn girl you've known ten minutes is in grave danger! So fuck the plan, fuck your colleagues and fuck me for vouching for you. Is that a fair—'

'...They're your "colleagues" and they can go to hell. I went there to prevent us dealing with a dead girl and—'

'*And yet somehow...*' Alexander leant forward and his sharp, angular features revealed themselves, deep shadows clawing at his profile. The voice filled the room, and the men looked across at him from the planes. '...Somehow, after your intervention, there were *three* dead bodies pulled from that hotel room.

'Now, I don't know, I have to go to the backers and explain what happened and... I'm at loss to articulate why we promise a swapped phone and some photographed documents from a safe, and we give them the Nite Owl Massacre. And now I have to go back and say, "I'm sorry everyone, you know that family friend I brought in to handle this? Yeah, he had a brain meltdown, and he ran in the hotel after a phone call from a twenty-three-year-old girl he was trying to fuck, and now she's dead, the person we actually sent to resolve the situation is dead and the hotel is swarming with English police. No, no, nothing to examine – just a gash-crazed pathetic old man that I insisted we hire."'

Under any other circumstances he would have laughed. He thought back to the evening Alexander came to see him. He thought back further to his lunch with Taisia. Perhaps, he mused as the human fist behind him pressed a gun into his head, this was all a sign that he that he had lived too long anyway; that it would have been better if he had died in the plane crash in the Congo.

Alexander had more to say: 'Or maybe, just maybe, there is another explanation. Now there are even some...

impartial observers, Mikhail, who would look at what just happened and might conclude that you had another agenda. They might conclude that someone else was paying you to sabotage the plan, to sabotage me.'

This was so unexpected, so insane, that he actually turned around and faced Alexander. 'What? Is that what you think?' He laughed incredulously. 'Is that really what you think?' He nodded over to the other men by the remaining plane. 'I don't know, Alexander, I think you've been spending too much time with your fag posse over there. I feel like I should have picked up on this earlier and staged some sort of… what's the word… intervention.'

There was silence, broken only by the distance shouts from the other men.

'The Arab you sent to clean the room—'

'May he forever rest in peace.'

'The one you didn't deign to tell me about…' he wasn't looking up at his darkened interlocutor now and he was staring blankly ahead at the planes being packed, 'took a sledgehammer to the problem, took it into his head to try to stab the girl.'

Silence. He didn't know what he had expected. A gasp of moral outrage, perhaps. Admittedly, he did feel stupid for not seeing it; it was, upon reflection, an admirable solution to a calamity – send in a wild-card headcase to eliminate any witnesses and who then could be blamed for everything. A very satisfactory solution if you disregarded the tally of dead women.

He said to Alexander, 'But then I feel like I'm not

telling you anything you didn't already know before I stumbled in.'

A murmur from Alexander. 'Funny. But we're no closer to understanding, "Why?" Why did you of all people decided to play Mother Theresa of the fucking Mayflower?'

Mikhail looked at the whimpering girl and shrugged. 'Do you always know why you do things, Alexander?'

For a brief, final moment their shared bond was revived and Alexander permitted himself a half-smile of acknowledgment.

Florentina was still clinging to his arm, and suddenly she stirred, lifted her head and squinted into the glare.

Sergei had walked over and retrieved the phone from the ground.

'She's not just some porn girl.' Her voice was hoarse and barely carried across the still air of the hangar. She stood up as tall as she could and tried to talk more, but her body strained at the physical effort.

'You didn't know… didn't…' Her voice was shaking again. '…Didn't care about how she…' The whir of the first plane's engine starting drowned out the rest of the encomium.

Alexander turned away and began the descent to floor of the hangar. As he reached the last of the stairs the plane began to roll forward. He tightened his grip on Florentina's arm. The stairs cast a shadow against the fluorescent empty space and Alexander's face was obscured in a pocket of darkness as the first plane taxied between them.

The whine and whir of the engine made any conversation impossible. Cinderblock and Bulldog had gone over to the second plane to help load the last of the crates. The first plane crossed the threshold and turned into the early cerulean dawn. The engine died down to a low buzz like a lawnmower.

Alexander walked towards them slowly and deliberately, each step a careful heel-toe placement that echoed crisply across the hangar. His face was neutral, expressionless. Florentina was looking at Alexander helplessly, expectantly, like she was waiting for him to pour out some expression of grief and horror as she had done. But Alexander could not, after all, be expected to express what he did not feel.

The girl let go of his arm and spoke first, pathetically: 'Alexander, I'm so sorry… It's all my fault.' She started weeping. Alexander ignored her and kept staring at him. Mikhail searched his face for traces of the boy he had known.

Mikhail finally spoke: 'The phone's SIM card has been replaced. I took out the Prince's card and replaced it with mine. It's back at the hotel. Think Michael Corleone and Sollozzo. When I've placed her on a plane – not you, or anyone else: me – then I'll tell you where to find it.'

The faintest smile from Alexander, and then there was another scream.

One of the Spetsnaz men had put a gun to her head. The panic and tension shot through him as she cried again in terror. His eyes flicked to the body bags and back to Alexander.

He turned to the Spetsnaz man, stepped forward quickly and grabbed Florentina's upper arm : 'Point the gun at me, point it at me!' He was so focused on the man, hissing at him through gritted teeth, that he didn't notice the second man pointing a gun at his own head.

Alexander: 'You at least have to have some sympathy for me, Mikhail. I talked everyone's ear off about how they have to bring in Mikhail, Mikhail is exactly who we need for something like this, blah, blah, blah. And now, now I'm left with this…' He gestured to Florentina, who was whimpering, 'Please, please, please, please!'

'Florentina…' The girl's articulation fell away, merging into a low mewl of terror and horror. '…Florentina, it's going to be OK – remember, just breathe in and out deeply. It'll be OK. Remember our chess game back at the hotel? Remember what we talked about?' She covered her face with her hands and continued with her gibberish pleading.

He turned his head to Alexander, looking past the gun barrel into the adamantine expressionless eyes.

'Florentina, my beauty.' He spoke to her soothingly, crisply. '…What happened to the SIM card?'

His stomach churned and he stared at the smooth grey concrete floor. Florentina didn't reply.

'Alexander, there's no value in doing this. The girl has much more value to us, to you, alive.' Mikhail felt the awful icy constriction in his chest again. Another cry of terror came from behind him, but he remained fixed on Alexander. Again, Alexander's head was tilted slightly to the side, like he was an emissary from an alien race observing human beings for the first time. His eyes flicked to Mikhail, who heard himself talking rapidly: '…There's no need, no value. Leave her alive and I'll come work for you, work for whoever you want to assign me to. Who knows the supply chain better than me? Who else knows that the fulfilment centres in Estonia don't actually scan most of their outbound packages into the overall system? Who else knows that customs at Haidar Pasha can't afford to assign anyone to check to containers?'

Hard to know whether this sales pitch would make any difference at all. He was so tired – not even the banal fatigue from lack of sleep, but an existential exhaustion, like the atmospheric pressure had concentrated and was forcing him down into the earth. Words continuing to be written after what should have been the final full stop.

'Alexander, let the girl go. You can do what you want to me. I'm ready. But let the girl leave. She's nothing, what purpose would it serve... doing anything else?' And one final, desperate plea: 'I knew your mother, she, she wouldn't want you doing this – not to her.'

Alexander's expression hadn't changed. 'Florentina...' His honeyed voice rolled gently through the hangar. '... Florentina, just tell me what Mikhail did with the SIM card, and this will all be over. You can go home.' In the far distance he could hear another plane landing. Outside the jade rays of the very early dawn could be seen breaking through the silver clouds. A nice scene to admire for the remaining seconds of his life.

The girl's small voice: 'I don't know. Please, I don't know. When we were at the hotel, he made me give him the phone, and then he left me alone for like ten minutes at the pool. Please, Alexander, I swear to God, I swear that's all I know.'

In that moment, in that second, he loved her.

There was another long, long silence. She was too far away for him to reach out and take her hand. He felt a cosmic sense of pride. As he kept his eyes locked downwards he allowed himself an invisible, inward smile. The chirp of some birds came to him as they glided past the hangar entrance. His eyes lost focus and he realised that there was nothing more he could do or say.

'So how many containers can we get through this port?'

And in an instant the weight was lifted. Alexander nodded to the Spetsnaz men and they dropped their guns.

Mikhail dropped to his knees and exhaled. There was a crumpled thud as Florentina fainted. He ran over to her and cradled her head. Her skin was very pale, cold and clammy, and the image of Taisia's death mask flashed through his memory.

Florentina eyes rolled back as he tried to slowly drag her up into a sitting position. He knelt back down on one knee – his bad knee – and winced in pain. 'You're OK… Florentina… we're OK.' A surreal lightheadedness seized him as he talked. She slurred something and he leant forwards to try to decipher what she was saying. Her voice was barely audible.

'…Can you… can you… can you ask for them… to pay Taisia's share to me… I can make sure it gets… make sure that it's used for Lada.' He bowed his head for a moment. The lacerating, hopeless feeling punctured his relief.

He looked upwards at Alexander. 'Get her the money – both hers and Taisia's. Right now. Get the full amount for both of them, and then double it. Take it from what you stole from the Prince. You can debit it against my future earnings.' He looked back down to her. 'How much did they promise they would pay you?'

'Thirty thousand. Each. It was meant to be in American dollars.'

He went to turn back to Alexander, but she had more to say: '...I don't actually know how much they were paying her.' Again, he felt the sorrowful, lacerating pain in his stomach. Such a pathetic, insignificant amount. His head had started to hurt, a gnawing, pulsating sensation in his temple.

'All that for thirty thousand, Alexander? Seems like a terrible waste.'

'We'll be sure to have a minute's reflection at the appropriate time.'

'Get them...' He paused while he tried to place an acceptable financial value on the terrible human wreckage from the evening, and he thought of the Arab bodyguard in the hotel lobby stuffing the fistfuls of bills into his jacket. '...Get her two hundred and fifty thousand – and another two hundred and fifty thousand for Taisia's daughter. American dollars.'

Alexander raised his eyebrows.

'Ha! Fuck off!' Sergei had re-emerged from the shadows and looked down mockingly from the catwalk. 'It's almost admirable, the *audacity*! Thirty seconds ago you both had a gun to your head, and now...' He was laughing quite hard. '...Now, after completely, completely fucking up a very basic task, you demand twenty times

– *twenty times* – your fucking salary. You should each be running a bank.'

Mikhail grabbed Florentina's arm and, as gently as he could, lifted her up to her feet. She staggered to the left, and he had to snatch at her arm again to keep her upright. He could feel Alexander's reptilian eyes upon them both. He turned back to face him and tried to raise himself up to his full height, but Florentina had hooked his elbow with her arms and she dragged him back down.

'Alexander, I know you have the money, those fucking Arabs were spilling it everywhere in that hotel. I saw it with my own eyes.'

'We've been over your excursion to the hotel.'

Alexander crossed his arms and apprised them. Finally he turned to Sergei: 'Go and get them two hundred thousand.' He looked faintly amused, as if he had engineered the request as some private joke.

For the briefest of moments, Mikhail considered remonstrating with him and demanding the amount he had requested. But he kept silent. Sergei again re-appeared from the darkness above them. He tossed two wads of American bills down, and they slapped the floor in front of Mikhail and Florentina.

'Well, you may as well take charge of her, after you went to all that trouble.' Alexander briefly inclined his head towards the rubble of the girl. Then he looked at Mikhail in the eye for an instant and then turned and walked away.

The second plane's engine rumbled to life, and he could feel its vibration in the air. The girl leant against his shoulder and he put his arm around her awkwardly, touching her outer arm and then jerking it away in embarrassment, letting it hover in the air. He looked up and saw Sergei and Yuri climbing up the compact metallic folding stairs into the cabin.

Alexander motioned to the stairs. 'Be my guests. Before the police arrive,' he shouted as the roar of the engine filled the hangar.

The girl tucked at Mikhail's arm urgently, but he didn't need to turn around. He took a step forward and shouted over the noise, 'We'll make our own arrangements to leave; you'll get me when you get me.'

Alexander looked at him levelly, and then he turned around. In her renewed terror Florentina had dug her fingers deeply into his arm and he winced as he extracted them. He clasped her hands, looked at her commandingly, and breathed in and out deeply until she followed his lead.

He looked back to the plane; Alexander was mounting the stairs whilst reading his phone.

When he reached the top stair Yuri turned around and motioned to Alexander, and then pointed to Mikhail and Florentina. A fleeting glance upwards, then a shake of the head. The three men disappeared into the cabin and the stairs rose slowly upwards.

For a few seconds he stood wondering when and how he would be prevailed upon to start settling the debt he had just incurred. Then Florentina lifted her head and he began to shepherd her slowly towards the rear exit, the two of them resuming their crustacean shuffle. The plane began to inch forward across the floor towards the slash of cerulean sky.

As they limped along, the girl let her head droop down and she dragged her bare feet along the glassy, reflective floor. Florentina tripped over her feet and his knee almost gave way as he fought to keep them upright.

She mumbled, 'Mikhail. I was trying so hard… I was trying… like you said… when you made me play chess… I was trying but… but I was so—' Her lips were quivering and he cut her off.

'It's OK, it's OK…' He exhaled deeply, tried to speak, but then he had a coughing fit. He coughed deeply and painfully, the burning, searing ice in his throat.

He looked back as he forced open the door as the second plane rolled out of the hangar and began to taxi right towards the runway. The two of them fell through into the cool, still air.

He bent forward and he had to let her go; they both fell to the ground. He rolled over onto his back and looked up at the glaring, blinding external lights of the hangar. He closed his eyes. It hurt to breathe, but he had to speak. He rolled over and looked at her. 'You…' – he exhaled, and it felt like his lungs were being dragged over broken glass – 'did…' – more pain – 'brilliantly.' He let his head fall until his forehead touched the concrete and he counted to forty-five.

Florentina lay on her side on the ground and curled her body into a ball. Mikhail was on his knees beside her. The first rays of the sun had just broken through the dark grey clouds. He closed his eyes and placed his hands on his hips.

Finally, the party was over.

2

THE OLD PILOT looked very concerned. Throughout their conversation his speech had halted several times, he had repeated himself, he had never looked directly at Mikhail, only at her. Mikhail trusted him immediately, although he knew how foolhardy that was. His co-pilot was much younger and when they first arrived he was occupied with the refuelling hoses.

The plane was an ATR: twin-engine, cargo-only, flying to Frankfurt, where (he assumed) it was subcontracted to one or more of the bigger corporate freight companies. He had deputised Florentina to monitor the story feed on the BBC website ('"Massacre": Three bodies found in Mayflower Hotel luxury suite – live updates'), but when he looked over she was desultorily swiping through Facebook photos of Taisia. Once again he had to stop himself from rounding on her; when the pilot returned to speak to him he was caught mid-swivel, positioned awkwardly between them. He wanted to rip the phone out of her hand, but for appearance's sake he rotated back to the right to listen to the pilot.

'Uh…' the pilot had crossed back over to them and his colleague stood behind him with his arms folded, 'Gaz and me, we, uh, we're really pressed for time here… we don't, um, we don't, we can't get involved in whatever it is with you two—'

'Then just take girl. She is being called Florentina.' He stepped to her and grabbed her by the arm, and she looked down at the ground vacantly. '…Please, I know you no take passenger as usual, but please, she is in much trouble. She is needing to leave England.' His conversation with Alexander was less an ironclad accord and more of a provisional truce, that, depending on the emergence of certain circumstances, say (to take a random example), Florentina talking to the English police, could be swiftly repudiated.

He spoke to her in Russian: 'Florentina, tell them, tell them you need to get home to Moscow to see your daughter…' He held up his right hand at waist height when she tried to interrupt. '…Tell them that there are people who are going to hurt you if you don't leave England immediately… And tell them…' He looked anxiously at the two pilots. '…Tell them, for the love of God, that it wasn't me that gave you the black eye.'

She reached up and touched her eye, which was black and blue and green, and almost swollen shut. He reflected that they now only had one working set of eyes between them. The pilots were both there now and he realised that he hadn't broached the subject of money yet. 'Florentina…' he said. The sound of his voice hung in the air for a few seconds. He wanted to prompt her again, but he couldn't bring himself to needle her after she'd done so well back in the hangar.

The pilots were now standing side by side staring at them both with crossed arms. He patted his jacket pocket for the ten thousand pounds he had extracted from the fistful of the Prince's money.

The girl still hadn't said anything and the men both took a step back when they saw the money. The younger one – 'Gaz' – started to laugh in disbelief, and the old pilot turned to him and raised his eyebrows, lost for words.

'It's your plane, Tom. I just work on it.' Gaz held up his hands, smiling, and he backed away and went back to the plane. Tom shook his head and he looked at the two Russians in confusion.

The four of them stood there in suspended animation, Mikhail holding the brick of money outstretched. Finally, Florentina spoke: 'My English… is… not so good. This, Mikhail, he… my friend, he *is* my friend… he help me when I very, very… sorry…' Her voice caught and she couldn't continue; the two pilots looked uncomfortable. 'Please… can you give help?' Shrunken, beaten, tired, makeup smeared, barefoot. It was like seeing a lamb caught in a bear trap, and he saw Gaz wince.

Tom and Gaz turned away and conferred in very low voices. He gripped Florentina's arm tighter and squeezed the money in his other hand, doing his utmost to channel the tension in his body. More seconds flowed by as the whispered conversation reached a crescendo. Tom came back over to them.

'Listen...' He halted again. '...I'm sorry, but we could only take one of you – we're freight, y'know, um, we're just not set up to take extra passengers. I'm sorry.'

Mikhail looked at Florentina and then said to Tom, 'Thank you, if you can just take her—'

The girl grabbed his arm with both hands: 'No! What about you?! You have to come!'

He looked at her, was about to speak to her, but instead he said to Tom. 'She will go. If you can take her to Frankfurt that will be enough. She can get home from there.' She tightened her grip and tried to drag his attention away from the pilots, but he shook her off. Gaz frowned with impatience and shifted from side to side.

'Tom...' He felt their relationship had progressed to the familiar level. '...If you can be taking her, only her...' He didn't have any further words left he could say. The Prince's money was still in his outstretched hand, and they both glanced down at it at the same time.

'Listen, put that away, put that away...' He batted Mikhail's hand away. He turned to Gaz. 'Are you gonna you be paid to work or to stand there gawkin'?'

Gaz shrugged. 'Plane's almost ready, boss. You and I have to collect those last pallets,' he jerked his thumb back to the plane, 'and we have the overflow stuff from the GLD Log guys left out on the runway that we have to load... then I just need to know how many people to put on the manifest.'

Tom bit his lip and took a long, long look at Florentina. At last he said, 'Well, can you wait outside for a few minutes? Gaz and me, we won't be long here. We have to do a final check and then we'll bring the plane outside as there's some stuff to be loaded outside before takeoff.'

Mikhail nodded. He said, 'Thank you. We can wait outside.' Tom nodded.

Florentina hissed, '*Mikhail!* You have to come! Tell him that y—' He seized her and marched her back out into the open cold air.

The lights of the runway floated against the white orange explosion of the coming dawn twilight. The two of them walked out a little way from the hangar and stopped near the neat pile of metal boxes stacked at the base of the closest airfield light. She tried to speak, but he cut her off harshly and made her give him the phone; he checked the updates:

4:10am: Multiple Metropolitan Police forensics teams have been dispatched to the Mayflower Hotel. A spokesperson for KRC International, which now owns and operates the Mayflower, has made the following comment:

'*We are shocked and horrified at the terrible events of the past evening, and stress that every effort is being made to assist the ongoing police investigation. We are working to relocate our guests to suitable alternate accommodation nearby.*'

One of the victims is believed to be Ghalib bin Kattan, an adviser to Prince Farouk Aziz Bin Fahd. As reported earlier, Prince Fahd was earlier tonight himself the victim of a sensational armed robbery whilst travelling through Luton after apparently fleeing the Mayflower Hotel.

The second victim has been identified as Tochukwu

Aniefuna, a bodyguard and valet to Prince Fahd. The identity of the female victim is yet to be released.

There were more updates, but he didn't want to read anything further. He let his arm drop to his side and stepped aimlessly in a semicircle. He closed his eyes and opened them, letting his vision stay blurred, unfocused. The runway lights each shattered into a thousand glittering rays, piercing the aquamarine gloaming that shrouded the airfield.

He tried to conjure her furious, beautiful, animated face from their first meeting in the café, the delicate, uncomprehending doll staring at the Polly Pocket. But he couldn't fix his mind upon any image that wasn't supplanted by the vacant, lifeless eyes staring through him into meaningless infinity.

'Mikhail...'

Florentina's voice broke into his thoughts and he looked up at her. Grey shadows ran across the crevices of her tired, injured face; in the weak, jaded light her body appeared as a darkened cerulean smudge against the floating golden lights.

'Mikhail! You don't have a way of getting *home*! You have to tell them!' Florentina's silhouette hissed at him again.

In the distance the red taxi lights of another, larger cargo jet smouldered through the mist as it began to roll towards the top of the far runway. He was watching it move as he walked over to her.

'Mikhail, when they're ready, we'll tell them they have to take you as well and—'

Once again he seized her, gripping each shoulder and shaking the poor girl furiously. 'I can organise myself.' Again he spoke harshly through gritted teeth; again she shrunk back. '...I don't need *you* to worry about *me*, I need you to get on that plane alone and then...' Florentina was shaking with terror, her head tilted to the side once again, and her eyes were vacant. He saw what he was doing, and he hated himself. Worse still, he had wasted valuable seconds on unleashing futile, pointless rage upon a suffering innocent.

'Listen... Florentina.' He removed his hands from her shoulders, but she kept her arms tucked in defensively to her body. 'I'm sorry. I'm so sorry. Listen...' He had to start with the easy part. He retrieved her passport and pressed it into her hand. 'Now...' The cargo jet started its sprint down the runway, its huge bulk gathering speed, carving through the fog and lifting into the morning sky. They both watched in silence for a few moments.

'Now,' he resumed. '...Now, when you get to Frankfurt, don't, I repeat, don't... you listening?' She nodded ever so slightly, but she didn't say anything and her mouth had fallen open in a parallelogram of terror. 'When you get to Frankfurt, *do not* get on another plane. I want you to take the train back to Moscow. I don't care how long it takes or have many separate trains you have to get on. Only show your passport if it's absolutely necessary. You understand?'

The morning air was very cold and the girl had started to shake again. He realised he should stop and give her his jacket, but he had too much to say. '*Do you understand what I just said to you?!'* Her head rolled round in what might have been a nod.

'Repeat what I just said to you.'

Her mouth was still hanging open, and her bare, thin arms had become very pale. He squeezed her arm and she focused her eyes, her lower jaw moving up and down silently like a fish. He didn't prompt her, just kept his eye locked on her until she managed, 'T-t-t-take the plane to F-F-F-F-Frank Frankfurt…'

He made to take off his jacket and put it around her but, reflecting that it was still stained with the Arab's blood, he thought better of it. He commanded her to continue, and she kept stammering, 'G-g-go on the train, not the p-plane… don't show my passport unless … Ihaveto.' The last words were choked out of her.

'And if the authorities ask you about what happened tonight, what do you say?'

A blank, nervous, searching expression. 'I-I-I don't know.' Florentina looked anguished.

'You say, "I can't help you. I was never there." And you say that over and over and over until they leave you alone. Now…' A familiar low, rumbling sound from the hangar and he whirled around to look at the warm, amber light streaming out into the blue dawn. After a moment, Gaz appeared and held up two fingers and then vanished back inside.

Something occurred to him: 'Do you still have the SIM card in your bra?'

The phrasing lacked elegance, and he immediately braced for the retort, but she slipped her hand into her dress without protest and handed him the tiny blue and gold rectangle. He took it between his thumb and forefinger and held it up to the light. For a second he beheld it as if it was a rare diamond before he placed it in his pocket.

He was still holding her left arm tightly and now he seized her other shoulder. 'Now, listen to me because this is the most important thing I have to say to you.' The noise increased as the nose of the plane emerged from the hangar.

He raised his voice and yelled desperately, 'Now, look at me and listen carefully to what I have to say now. Look at me!' He squeezed her arm and her shoulder until she cried in pain. His shadow cut diagonally across her small, frightened, sallow face. The left eye was now a terrible blackened slit and her lips had become tinged with blue. Her right eye was expanded in fright.

'Taisia's daughter. She's your responsibility now. You're her mother now, do you understand?' The plane was now creeping slowly up the tarmac towards them. The drone of the engine was growing louder and louder and louder, and his panic rose and rose because he didn't think she understood the import of what he had just said.

'Florentina. Do you understand what I'm saying to you?' The plane was bearing down on them steadily. The taxi lights illuminated the grey wings and dull fuselage. It rolled to a stop beside them, the door unhatched and the ladder descended, and the rear flap opened slowly.

He looked back at the girl. 'Florentina, I need you to say it.' The taxi lights threw a deep red cast across her anguished expression. She locked and unlocked her skittering fingers. The whir subsided as the engine wound down and Gaz and Tom clambered down onto the tarmac. Tom glanced at them as the two men hurried over and each took a handle of the first silver metal box. They puffed and strained as they lurched across the concrete plain and up into the hold. He felt ashamed that he wasn't helping, standing to the side like a useless fairy. But he hadn't finished what he needed to say.

'Florentina.' He stepped right up to her so that she had to crane her neck backwards to look at him. 'You're a mother now and I need you to say you're a mother.' A flash of Taisia outside the café shouting and wailing down the phone at the phantom ex-boyfriend.

'B-b-but Taisia's… mama…' Tom and Gaz huffed their way past with the other large box. Only one large rectangular box, and two much smaller boxes, remained. '…Lada… she stays with Taisia's mama, she knows Lada… I wouldn't even know…'

He rounded on her: 'Yes, because she had such success keeping Taisia on the right path! Some old babushka who couldn't stop her daughter falling in with men who didn't care whether she lived or died. What's she going to do? What? What!' Poor woman, really. But he continued: '… Now…' Florentina's face had fallen further and tears had re-appeared in her eyes. Her forehead was lined and blue. 'I'm, I'm…' – gape, gape – 'I'm only nineteen… And there's no goddamn fucking point to… anything… Mikhail, I'm useless, I'd be useless… I don't know…'

'You *do* know, Florentina…' The two pilots ran past them to fetch the final two boxes and Tom motioned to them. Mikhail looked at the old pilot and inclined his head very briefly, but he kept his hands gripped tightly on the girl. '…You do know because you've seen it. What happened tonight – you saw it, you saw it – and you know that if you don't take care of that girl, nobody else will. Now…' He gritted his teeth hard and placed his face as close to hers as was possible. '*Say. It.*'

Her head rotated slowly and then stopped. And then, unexpectedly, mercifully, she fixed him with a focused, resolute expression, and she said, 'I'm a mother. Lada. Lada is my daughter.'

The plane's engine jumped to life, and in the corner of his eye he saw Tom waiting beside the ladder. A wall of mechanical sound crashed over them. There was one last thing. He shouted at her, '*And one last thing. How do I find you on Instagram? So I know that you're safe?*'

She looked at him uncomprehendingly for a moment. Then she stood on her toes and, with a great effort, she grabbed his shirt and yelled, '*Search for Florentina Fine – but with an underscore after Florentina.*' She rocked back onto her feet, but then she grabbed him desperately with her tiny blue hands and stood back on her toes and yelled, '*You have to use English characters, not Russian characters. Florentina underscore Fine – F-i-n-e!*'

He nodded at her. For the final time each looked at the other through their respective solitary working oculus. He wanted to try and say something, but he didn't know what. Suddenly she leant back up on the tips of her toes and threw her arms around him. Again he briefly encircled her body, gingerly touching her back very, very lightly for a second and then withdrawing his arms in embarrassment. She fell back and he turned her around, pushing her gently towards the plane.

Florentina struggled to balance on her bare toes, lifting each foot straight up and then stabbing it down as if she were stepping over broken glass. Tom hurried forward with his arm outstretched and grabbed her before she stumbled again. With surprising strength he swept her up and carried her the last few metres to the stairs.

Gaz appeared at through the hatch and took her left arm as she clambered up the last of the stairs. Florentina turned and looked down at him from the top of the stairs. The towering lights shone down and the bright white glow ringed her head and pulled at the shadows below her eyes.

She held up her slender pale arm and waved at him weakly. He had his arms crossed and he stared back at her sternly. It would have been better to wave back or nod to her, but his thoughts were already fixed upon Taisia. There would be a swarm of police crawling in and out of the suite now. Photographing and measuring and scraping and poking at her. And then zipping her into some plastic bag and depositing her in a silent, subterranean hospital chamber. Florentina had looked at him uncertainly for a few seconds before Tom had placed his hand gently on her shoulder and she had turned around and she was gone. The end of a beautiful friendship, he thought, darkly.

Tom followed her inside and a moment later the stairs began to arc upwards through the air until the fuselage was sealed. The plane started to move forward almost immediately. Mikhail stood watching it as it made its way to the head of the runway.

There was an emptiness inside him now, but also a roiling, terrible confusion. A brief image of Alexander looking at him down from above as the guns were pressed to their heads, which he banished immediately. He felt ashamed as the dark, hopeless feeling of loss pressed down upon him. So he had been reduced, finally, to this: standing alone in the dawn in a state of mourning for a woman he had barely known, wild with concern for her daughter whom he would never meet and wouldn't know that he existed, betrayed by the man he thought of as family. And, of course, dependent upon a young student's Instagram account as his window on the world.

He was a shipwreck survivor cast upon an endless sea. The plane was waiting at the head of the adjacent runway. There was a short, coiled silence and then it burst forward; his head moved quickly to the right as he watched it accelerate faster and faster and then finally levitate through the grey-blue sky. It rose higher and further until it was swallowed by the clouds.

For a long minute he stood alone staring at the space between the clouds where she had vanished. He breathed in deeply and breathed out.

And then he walked back across the tarmac.

ACKNOWLEDGEMENTS

I would like to thank my brother Gavin and my sister Miranda for their support. I would also like to thank Patrick Loyatum, the Garrard family, and Matt Baillie for their enthusiasm for my work. Lastly I would like to thank the Book Guild for taking a chance on this book.